Three Loves

by

Mike Silkstone

UNDEAD TREE

Copyright © Mike Silkstone, 2011.

Undead Tree Publications
9 Normanby Terrace, Whitby, North Yorkshire, YO21 3ES, England.
http://www.undeadtree.com

All Rights Reserved.

No part of this publication may be reproduced, stored in a retrieval system, or transmitted in any form or by any means, electronic, mechanical, photocopying, recording or otherwise without the prior written consent of the publisher or the copyright holder, or a licence for copying in the UK issued by the Copyright Licensing Agency Ltd, 90 Tottenham Court Road, London W1P 9HE.

With the exception of major historical figures, all characters are entirely fictitious. Any similarity with persons living or dead is purely coincidental.

ISBN 978-1-898728-22-1

2 3 4 5 6 7 8 9

Set in Garamond by Undead Tree Publications.
Printed and distributed worldwide by Lulu.com

Contents

Prologue 5
Chapter 1 9
Chapter 2 15
Chapter 3 19
Chapter 4 29
Chapter 5 33
Chapter 6 37
Chapter 7 45
Chapter 8 57
Chapter 9 65
Chapter 10 73
Chapter 11 79
Chapter 12 83
Chapter 13 93
Chapter 14 99
Chapter 15 107
Chapter 16 111
Chapter 17 119
Chapter 18 129
Chapter 19 133
Chapter 20 143
Chapter 21 147
Chapter 22 153
Chapter 23 161
Chapter 24 165
Chapter 25 169
Epilogue 175

To Trevor, Mum, Ivan, Monty and Poll-Doll.

Prologue

1790

"Come on, lad, waken up."

The boy blinked in the yellow glow of the lamp, as an impatient parent insisted, "No time to dawdle, we need to be away, and quick."

Still only half-dressed, he was carried out of the cottage and lifted into the back of the cart, along with whatever possessions had been hurriedly assembled for this midnight exodus.

And now, wide awake, Tom asked, "Where's mother?"

The man looked away. "She's dead."

Father and son clung to each other and the man wept.

"That's why we need to get started," Ben Metcalfe said through his tears. "So much sickness—we mun be well away from 'ere afore daybreak."

Tom pointed to his sister curled up in a blanket, already asleep and sucking her thumb. "Does Leah know?" His father shook his head. "Now, the sooner we get on the high road afore we're discovered, the better."

Tom glanced back at what until minutes ago had been their home, and saw a sudden brightness in the windows. His nostrils caught a whiff of smoke as he saw the first of the flames creep up the thatched roof.

"The house—it's on fire!"

"Aye, and we mun let folks think we perished in the flames. Then they'll not hunt us down, thinkin' we're spreadin' the plague." And with a new sense of urgency Ben Metcalfe cast a farewell glance over his shoulder, then began leading the horses along the lane toward the high road.

The cart creaked, its clumsily-fashioned wheels rattled noisily over the hard-baked ruttle track, the night sounds being disturbed by the clip-clop of the horses' hooves and the jangle their belongings made as they rattled against one another before settling down. While sullying the sweet night air was an acrid smoke and showers of sparks as flames reached up towards the heavens to cover their escape.

Tom looked back. Everything he'd grown up with would soon be charred ruins. Thoughts were racing through his young mind. Where were they going? What was to happen to them? Would they return when the plague had died down? But... to what?

And if they were fleeing, then what about the rest of the villagers? For it seemed to Tom that everyone had been afflicted, hence the fields of unharvested crops and cottage gardens full of rotting fruit, cattle straying and breaking down fences.

The plague must have even reached the manor house, for his father had returned from there only that afternoon with the candlesticks and other things wrapped in fine linen and carried close inside his jacket. Tom had seen them as they were later laid out on the table being "appraised", alongside the gun his father kept close to him while he stared first at the loot, then at the door.

He must have known then that they were about to flit, or why would he have done such a terrible thing? Unless it was because of which they were now fleeing? Tom supposed the things would be hidden in the cart with the rest of their belongings.

At sunrise the early morning mist began to clear. By then they were well beyond the city limits. Tom and Leah watched the towers of the Minster melt into the distance, as hour by hour they put mile upon mile between the life they were leaving behind, and drawing closer to their new one, whatever it was to be.

At the next toll gate the gatekeeper gave them curious looks, and as they approached the nearby village they were met with hostility and stone-throwing. Hungry and weary they travelled on.

The second day saw Tom leading the horses and Leah straddling the mare, whilst in the back of the cart, suddenly fallen ill, lay the man who had engineered their escape.

Tom stopped at the first ale house to buy bread and refreshment, and as he held the tankard to his father's lips he was given instructions regarding their ultimate destination, and the name of the person to seek out on their arrival.

They were heading toward the seaport town of Whitby, to the home of Nathaniel Stottard, their father's cousin. Once under his protection all would be well, Tom was assured. For he was an apothecary and would be able to cure the illness afflicting the man giving instructions but now fading fast.

Tom listened carefully. Hidden in the cart were documents to prove their identity, and also the pistol in case they were set upon. On no account were they to halt or for any reason abandon their journey, for they had nothing to return to. Their escape—and the burning of their cottage—had given them a new life, but it had also claimed their old one.

Later that day their cart was stopped by two rough-looking villains who would have ransacked their possessions, had it not been for the sight of the dying man.

"The plague!"—one of them mouthed the words as he recoiled in horror.

"Then let's away," his companion muttered through clenched teeth, a protective hand across his mouth.

Tom, his arms still round his sister, watched the two men hurriedly leave. Then he peered inside the cart, just as his father breathed his last.

With a woollen cloth for a shroud, the corpse was unfittingly laid to rest in a shallow ditch and covered with bracken fronds and clumps of heather. Tom uttered the only prayer he knew and, as brother and sister stood beside the makeshift grave, Leah, suddenly frightened by their being now alone, clung to her brother. And from the frail body of a twelve-year-old boy there emerged the strength and protection of a man—a child no longer.

"Don't worry, Leah, we'll soon be in Whitby. And I'll look after you—I'll always be there for you."

Had anyone asked where they had buried the body they could only have replied, "on the moors, somewhere between Pickering and the *Saltersgate Inn*, at the side of the pack-horse road."

At the next bridge they stopped and led the horses to the stream and ate some blackberries growing among the heather. All around them the purple hills sprawled as far as the eye could see, while at their feet, winding along insidiously, was the lonely salt road used by pack horses to transport the said mineral from mines in Cheshire to the coast, where it was used for preserving fish.

At first light the following day Tom hitched the horses to their cart and, as the moorland mist slowly dispersed, he began to question the good sense of this journey. Suppose their relative was indisposed toward them, or in dire need himself? Why—he could be dead, or have long ago moved to some other town. Whatever would they do then?

Momentarily tiring of her gew-gaws, and impatient to be moving on, Leah skipped between the single row of flagstones that traversed the moor while her brother deliberated on whether to continue or retrace their steps. "Come on, Tom," she called, her voice tinkling, feet beating the taut skin of the moorland peat.

In the distance she saw some flowers, and appearing quite unworried that they were now orphans, she began picking them as she waited for her new protector to hitch the horses to the cart.

That morning they met two other travellers, both riding mules, the woman red faced and jolly, the man with a bent nose and blue scars down his cheek. It would be several miles, they told them, before the abbey would be in sight. But from then on, and from every hill or vantage point, Tom surveyed the skyline.

Suddenly Leah pointed—to a kestrel seemingly suspended in the air, until it suddenly swooped down on its prey. Tom stared beyond the flight of the bird and beheld a welcome landmark: the end of their journey.

"Look, Leah! The abbey! We're nearly there. Before the day's out we'll be in Whitby."

With renewed enthusiasm they began the last part of their eventful journey, and as they came to the edge of the moor they saw to their right a tiny hamlet not unlike the one they'd left behind.

As they crossed the wooden bridge that spanned the river, Tom again wondered about their reception in Whitby. And as if in reply the sun came out from behind a cloud, spilling its rays across the river Esk, and Tom took it as a favourable omen. A new life was awaiting them.

He was a bright lad. He could read and write, and in a busy seaport this would surely be an advantage. He could perhaps learn to handle a boat. Why—he might even become a sea-captain.

While these and other half-formed thoughts whirled around in his brain, a man driving some cattle nodded to them and Tom asked "D'you live in these parts?"

The man nodded again, took the straw from his mouth and gave a well-measured spit. Then in reply to Tom's next question he drawled the words, "Apothecary? You'll want Church Street. Anyway, why d'you want an apothecary? You ailing, or summatt?"

"No," Leah piped up, "we're going to live there."

As her innocent remark struck home, Tom again questioned the good sense of this journey which was almost at an end. But, he reasoned, there was only one way now—and that was forward.

They were ready for their new life in Whitby.

But was Whitby ready for them?

Chapter 1

1804

With a feeling of pride Thomas Benjamin Metcalfe (or Tom, as he preferred to be known) paused from his Monday morning chores, straightened his back and gazed with pride at the neat well-stocked shelves of the shop.

Since first light he'd been busy re-arranging the counters, replenishing his store of herbs, placing fancy jars of a new pomander in the window, sweeping, dusting, polishing the brass apothecary scales, making sure the residents of the large blue and white jar were healthy so they would do what was required of them when needed—in short, attending to the endless tasks a shopkeeper needed to do.

The pungent smell of southernwood mingled with fragrant lavender assailed his nostrils and he inhaled deeply, savouring the aromas. Of all the varied smells in his shop Tom preferred southernwood, using it in hair lotions, *pot-pourri* and the various other concoctions he made up, then sold to his regular (and seemingly grateful) customers.

Whitby needed something sweet-smelling. For when the whaling ships returned and were in the harbour the air would be sullied for days with the heavy lingering stench of boiling blubber from the oil yards either side of the river.

There was also the ever-present smell from the nearby coaching inn of horses and stabling. From the many alleyways came that of privvies, plus the eternal smell of fish, and from every street corner the stink of urine which was used in the alum trade. All this mingled with the exotic aromas of the quayside: some foreign ship unloading her cargo, or the sweet-sour fumes of tarred hemp, canvas and linseed oil, the smell of new ropes; the summer heat, the flies, the rats and all the other vermin that came in on the boats.

But worst of all was the ever-present and putrid stench from the lant ships which, although moored out to sea, still made their presence felt.

Little wonder, then, that Tom's sweet-smelling wares were in such demand. For 'uncle Nathan', as the two orphans called their protector and benefactor, had taught Tom well.

Now the old man was almost sightless, with a confused and wandering mind, needing as much attention as a baby or stray kitten that Leah might take in and care for. This left Tom now in control of the business: his own master in this busy seaport town.

With Leah attending to the customers, and Walter Grainger, an old man who searched the hedgerows and regularly appeared with a hand-cart full of herbs and roots, they made a handsome living. Life was good—and Tom felt he and his sister had much to be grateful for.

A shaft of spring sunlight spilled through the window as Tom opened the shop door to the ever-present sound of the gulls and the rattle of a coach and horses. Further along Church Street he could see the impressive team of greys outside the *White Horse and Griffin*. This was the regular coach service to York which departed on alternate days from the *White Horse* or the *Turk's Head*.

No longer was Whitby an isolated community, for the town could also boast a regular diligence to nearby Scarborough on Sundays and Wednesdays. And there was also the Mail Coach which departed from the *Rose and Crown* in Leeds each evening, calling at Whitby or Scarborough on alternate days.

There was the busy port with whaling ships bound for Greenland, cargoes arriving regularly from the continent, even occasionally from as far away as China or the East Indies. There was the Custom House and, running hand-in-glove with the legitimate trade of the harbour, was the occasional smuggling vessel with its cargo of illicit brandy. And, on more than one occasion, 'baccy for Uncle Nathan.

Suddenly remembering the old man, Tom wiped his hands, took his fob-watch from his pocket and, casting a last glance round the shop, hurried through the back room and upstairs to their living quarters. Leah was already moving around. He could hear her laughter as she fussed over the new members of their family.

" 'Morning Tom. Come and look at Sukey. She's opened her eyes, she can see now. Oh, she's lovely, Tom."

Like small children, brother and sister bent over the basket containing the three kittens. Leah held the black and white ball of fluff in one hand while she gently stroked its baby velvet fur with the fingers of the other. As Tom knelt beside her, the mother cat came and rubbed herself against his knees.

"Martha's jealous."

"Oh no, she's not. She's proud of her lovely babies. And she's been fed. That was the first job I did, even before I started making our breakfasts."

Tom's thoughts turned to food. "What are we having?"

"Bread and cheese, or there's some fish. But I was saving that for Martha… unless you want—"

Tom saw the look of consternation on her face. "Bread an' cheese'll be fine…"

"And some gruel for uncle. Because now he's got no teeth, there's not a lot he can manage."

His sister fussed around, and they began their meal. She was just twenty-one and, as yet, unattached, but with her blonde hair and rosebud lips it was little wonder that all the young men flocked to her side, be it in church, or simply out for a stroll with her friend Constance Langden.

She read the look of unashamed admiration in her brother's eyes, then asked, in mock severity, "and just… what are you thinking, Tom Metcalfe?"

" I wor just…" and his mouth broke into creases of laughter at her expression.

"Come on, out with it."

"Just thinkin'…" and he slid his chair back from the table as she reached across and held the milk jug above his head, threatening him.

"Yes?"

"Thinkin'… " and he pulled a face as he felt the first trickle of milk on his chin. Then, in desperation, and so that he would not have to put on another clean shirt he blurted out, "thinking you might like some new gloves, or a bonnet," and he skilfully dodged her outstretched arms, and quickly moved further round the table.

"Gloves and bonnet?"

"Aye…" he finally relented. "Owt fer thee."

"No, Tom," she corrected him. "'Anything for you'. Or should it be 'for you, Leah, anything'. That's what you should say, and that's how you must always speak in the shop, or else people will think you're no better educated than that old frump from Salt-Pan-Well steps—and they'll buy their potions from her."

"They'll soon be back. There's many as had one of Ada-Martha so-called cures—and never recovered from it. Besides, it's only young lasses go to Ada-Martha's and we can do without that sort o' business."

Leah turned away, and Tom could see her colour rising. He quickly changed the subject.

"Is uncle awake?"

She nodded.

"Then I'll see if he's ready."

"Let's finish our breakfast first"—and Leah paused to offer a morsel of bread thickly smeared with butter to Martha, who was polishing her shoes with her fur. "Then you can get him dressed, and I'll get him fed."

A clock struck the hour. Tom swallowed his last mouthful then hurried from the table and across the hallway to attend to his morning ritual.

For the last two, nearly three, years his uncle had been in his own private world. Sometimes he could be quite sensible, but more often in a confused, but seemingly quite happy state. On bad days, especially when he was planning to assassinate King George, he was confined to his room, as he had been for most of the winter. He'd seemed quite determined to put an end to His Majesty and all his advisors, and on becoming quite excited and explicit had needed to be dosed with laudanum.

Why he should want to harm the King was something of a mystery, and Tom was relieved when spring arrived, and uncle Nathaniel found a new toy to amuse himself.

A drum.

He could sit in front of his bedroom window, and with the familiar sights and sounds of the harbour ever near could innocently pass away the hours banging out a monotonous, or at other times agitated, rhythm. Fortunately it turned his mind from thoughts of royal assassination.

"Mornin', uncle."

The frail figure in the four-poster, mouth gaping open, turned his head toward the sound. "Tom?"

" 'Ow's uncle this mornin'?" and Tom began the ritual of first helping him from his bed before leading him to, and sitting him on, the commode. As his gnarled hands and long cold fingers grasped the strong arms of his helper, he asked, "What day is it, Tom?"

"Monday. Now let's have a look at thee," and Tom saw the stained bedclothes and wet night-shirt. "Tha's 'ad another accident, uncle."

"I wor dreaming last night, Tom," the old man ignored the remark, "an' I wor in a cornfield wi' a lass called Molly. An'... I spanked 'er. I fair brought mi 'and across 'er bare bottom, an' then—"

"No bloody wonder tha pittled 'bed."

"Eh?"—and the rheumy near-blind eyes grew wide with innocence. The old man in the billowing night-shirt suddenly went off on another topic: "'Ow's t'war, Tom? Are we still fightin' Napoleon?"

"I'll tell thee all abaht that after I've finished cleanin' thee up."

Minutes later, ablutions completed and Tom leading the way, the two of them crossed the hallway and came into the kitchen. "Did yer say it wor Sunday, Tom? Are we goin' to church?"

"No, that wor yest'day. I told yer, when yer wor askin' abaht 'war."

"*War?* Are we at war?"

"Aye. Against Napoleon."

Leah held a spoonful of gruel to the old man's lips. "Come on, uncle, get this down before it goes all cold and lumpy."

"Is it nice?"

"Mmm. And I've poured some honey over it."

He managed no more than a few mouthfuls before waving a hand in protest. He began, "If Napoleon dares to invade, His Majesty will need a war-room close to the harbour. He shall stay with us."

"Aye."

As he rambled on, Tom looked at his sister, then said, "when Hannah arrives, uncle's bed needs seeing to, and… I mun open the shop."

"I'll lend a hand as soon as I can," and resuming her spoon-feeding, Leah begged, "Come on, uncle, I've stirred the honey in, just as you like it."

"I'd rather 'ave some porridge."

"It *is* porridge"—and she sighed as he again pushed the spoon away.

As Tom busied himself among his bottles and jars in his preparation room, the first of the morning's customers came and went. Colic mixture for the woman from Arguments Yard, and attar of roses for Miss Tiplady, an old spinster with a face mean as ditchwater.

No sooner had the coins for this transaction been grudgingly placed in his hands than an excited young woman's voice called from the doorway "Leah, Leah, he's back." The girl looked round inside, before asking the proprietor, "Where is she?"

"Upstairs—no, she's 'eard thee, she's—"

"Leah, *he's home!*"

"Who? Lynton?"

"No—Ashley!"

Leah, her face suddenly illuminated, gave a shriek of delight. And the two young women, caring little for the commotion they were creating, threw their arms round each other, and jumped and cavorted like silly schoolgirls.

Dark-haired Constance Langden saw Tom glaring in mock disapproval and she giggled as she tried to compose herself, before bursting forth with "Isn't it all too exciting, Tom! Ashley's home—well, he soon will be. He's coming in on the tide."

Tom's still wedge-bone face surveyed the now somewhat disarranged curls and sparkling eyes of the two girls. Leah, all bashful on hearing the news that her childhood sweetheart would soon be in town. And Constance, thrilled as only a sister could be, now her devoted brother had safely returned from his long sea voyage.

"We must go and meet him." Constance, some two years older than her friend, was already taking charge. "We shall go now and stand on the quayside, so's we'll be able to welcome him properly. Papa had letters from him while he was in London. He's got presents for us Leah—he said so. Oh, come on!"

"Oh... go on, then." For Tom knew he'd get precious little help in the shop until his sister had seen Ashley again, and as the girls stared at his intentionally pained expression, they both began giggling anew till he finally declared, "Damned silly creatures, women."

He and Leah, Ashley and Constance, the four of them had grown up together. Only days ago Tom had himself received a letter from Ashley informing him he would be arriving in Whitby as soon as a ship was available. He was as excited as the two girls, and several times that morning did he rush to the top of the house and stick his head out of the attic window that overlooked the harbour.

There seemed a veritable forest of ships' masts that poked and prodded the blue of the sky and the scurrying morning clouds, and he could well imagine the to-ing and fro-ing of the smaller craft that would be escorting Ashley's ship, and the activity at near-fever pitch as she began to unload.

Tom again envied the two young women who would by now be standing at the quayside, and could well imagine their yelling and screaming as they were caught up in the euphoria. They would be jumping up and down, arms round one another and squawking like parakeets, he didn't wonder.

But as even he had to admit, they'd be very pretty parakeets. Very pretty indeed.

Chapter 2

Ashley Langden, with the air of one well-travelled, smiled contentedly as he surveyed the boxes and packing cases which seemed to completely fill his cabin, the souvenirs and spoils of his latest and, he'd already decided, his last voyage.

His five years as ship's surgeon had certainly been colourful and at times traumatic. And at the ripe old age of twenty eight he'd seen, and done, more than enough.

On the occasions when he'd had to perform an amputation, he'd been nearly as terrified as the patient—and the piercing, near-demented screams of the poor devil strapped to the table had echoed and reverberated in his brain for days after such a piece of butchery. Then, assuming the patient had survived the mutilation and the cauterizing iron used to stem the bleeding, there would follow a raging fever and the very real risk of fatal infection in the angry inflamed stump.

It made a sorry picture, and had he known then when he was still learning and sharing a room with fellow student Lynton Shaw… but that was a long time ago.

Like brothers they had been, and quite inseparable. Lynton even accompanied him to Whitby during their Christmas and summer breaks. They studied together and helped each other understand anatomy and dissection of the human body.

Subsequently, they received their certificates from the Royal College of Surgeons on the same afternoon, and that evening, the worse for drink, Lynton confessed he was hopelessly in love with the other's sister, Constance.

"You and Connie? That's great news!" Looking up from his ale, and with more manners than was needed for the rough tavern they were frequenting, Ashley enquired, "And has she said 'yes'?"

Lynton Shaw sighed. "I haven't told her yet."

"Then you must, before some other fellow does. Damn it, man. I won't be cheated out of having you as a brother-in-law. What say you we spend a few days in Whitby?"

"We've till the end of the month," Lynton reminded him. "Now you've got your certificate from the East Indian Company's physician, you'll be due to sail the China Seas any day thereafter."

Ashley nodded gloomily. At twenty-five he'd been accepted as surgeon's mate: an appointment that filled him with a certain trepidation.

But Lynton's surprise revelation put all else from his mind, and the two of then decided to head for Whitby the following day.

A smiling Constance met the two young men and, several days later, waved her brother and her husband-to-be goodbye. Papa had raised no objections to Lynton's asking for her hand, and she now looked to the day when she would be Mrs Lynton Shaw.

The two young men returned to their London lodgings to find Ashley's sailing orders waiting for him, on a ship carrying close on a hundred and fifty men, four mates, captain, purser, a surgeon, and himself as surgeon's mate. This would be his first taste of life at sea proper.

Before sailing, and as part of his duties, he assisted the surgeon in checking the medicine chest and surgical equipment, and also making sure there were sufficient gallons of lime juice carried on board so as to ward off scurvy. As the barrels were being stowed away he recalled as an apprentice seeing the bleeding gums and ulcerations resulting from this complaint.

The following morning his own personal belongings (similar to that of a midshipman) came aboard. Hammock, hair mattress, pillow, wash-hand basin and cut-throat razor, together with medical books, surgical instruments, personal clothing and surgeon's-mate uniform. It was too late now to turn back, to have second thoughts.

He smiled as he remembered his maiden voyage, but swallowed hard as he thought of the sea sickness that had persisted till there was nothing left inside him, and he felt ready to breathe his last. Then he became accustomed to the constant roll of the ship and the wearisome pewter sea, and the very real difference in earning one's living instead of being a student, provided-for by an indulgent father.

Five days out, there had been a sudden storm. The sky was riven with lightning, and walls of salt spray tore across the deck, stinging and blinding. The vessel seemed to Ashley's inexperience to have as much chance on the open water as a chamber-pot.

How the ship survived he would never know, but the following morning the sun rose, painting the sea an ochreous yellow. While the more experienced members of the crew began making good the ravages of the storm, Ashley Langden yearned for dry land.

But, as in all things, there was a bright side for one in his position. Together with his monthly pay he was allowed, like all the officers, to engage in what was termed "private trading"—which meant that he could take goods with him to be sold on reaching their destination, and similar arrangements were made for the homeward voyage. While there were restrictions on items such as tea or silk, arsenic or other poisonous drugs, and a custom duty of three per-cent paid to the company for the warehousing of such goods, a handsome profit was still to be made.

Two years later, on being promoted to ship's surgeon proper, he was allowed to take up to six tons of merchandise, his stock including hosiery, hats, red lead, port wine and rolls of cloth.

On his first voyage he made over five hundred pounds profit. Taken together with his five pounds monthly wage as surgeon, his future looked bright—as bright as the crew did when the noon bell struck, and the ship's fifer blew his pipe to give notice that the daily measure of brandy was to be distributed.

On the darker side, he saw the cruelty that existed on board ship; the harsh punishments meted out by more than one sadistic captain; men keel-hauled, or the flesh torn from their bodies as they were flogged for some misdemeanour. Life at sea could be cruel.

Many times more cruel, however, was the necessary pain he had to inflict when amputating an arm or a leg crushed in some accident, or because of gangrene. The agonising screams, the stench of pus, the rotting flesh, the rasp of the saw before the limb fell off... then the stump would be dipped in boiling pitch to stem the flow of blood—and Ashley would think, "Poor bastard... poor unfortunate bastard!"

From early on he'd learned to make sure he had a good measure of brandy inside him before he started hacking away. As a small child when he'd seen among the sailors on the quayside the usual assortment of peg-legs or one-armed men, probably as a result of some whaling accident he'd never imagined that he could ever be called upon to perform such a mutilation.

Yet that was one of the first things he'd had to do: remove someone's hand. The young man's screams would live with him for the rest of his life. Several years and many amputated limbs later they were still with him, trapped in his brain forever.

But now, thanks to good voyages and profitable trading and the monthly pay he'd accumulated, he could say goodbye to the sea. For he had grown rich. His latest cargo from Canton included packages of gunpowder, mother-of-pearl beads, ivory, jade and rolls of cloth. And, stored away with his personal belongings were fine brocades for Constance, Chinese silverware, oriental vases and a most magnificent dinner service.

Fortune had been with him on his return voyage, despite storms and a puny threat from a French man-o'-war while they were still some miles from home, fear of pirates, and the constant threat from His Majesty's impress-men, who could upon production of a warrant forcibly board a ship and, interpreting the law to suit themselves, take whatever men they wanted. But Ashley was convinced that it was time to quit while things were still in his favour.

A short stay in London, as he waited for a ship to Whitby, had also made him realise something else: that it was time to end his "bachelor" status and put a stop to illicit love affairs as-and-when the occasion arose. So—honourable man that he was—he called at the most prestigious jewellers in Hatton Gardens to choose a diamond and emerald necklace as a betrothal gift. It was in one of his trunks, along with the fine clothes he'd had tailored for his new life.

As he took a last calculating look at the things in his cabin, he again grew restless, and his blond head peered through the porthole before he made his way up on deck. Ahead of him, and becoming clearer by the minute, was the familiar jut of land with the ruined abbey perched on top. He was home!

An air of expectancy and excitement ran through him. As the deckhands made ready to approach the harbour, Ashley rushed to the prow as the first vessels to greet them came within hailing distance. A veritable flotilla it seemed to him, composed of everything that could sail.

A fishing boat with as much free-load as a frying pan rocked dangerously to portside. As Ashley watched, fully expecting the next wave to submerge it, there was a respectful cough before, "Beggin' yer pardon, Sir."

He turned towards the voice. "Yes?"

"Your luggage, Sir?"

"Bring it up, all of it."

"And what about… the 'other thing', Sir? The one you said we was to take special good care of?"

"Good God!"—for Ashley in all the excitement had forgotten his friend. "Is he well?"

In answer to his question, a large, crudely constructed cage was brought up from below. The occupant gave a lethargic, non-committal "goodbye", then began rubbing his beak against the bars of his temporary home. Like all true seamen, Ashley had not been able to resist the urge to bring home an exotic bird as a reminder of his travels. Together with a wealth of tales to relate to his family, the yellow-and-blue macaw would serve as a permanent reminder of his years of sailing the China Seas.

But such fireside yarns could wait, for there was something much more important to do.

He had to find Leah Metcalfe and ask her to marry him.

Chapter 3

The home of James Langden was the scene of feverish activity that evening as a cook, chambermaid, butler and Maria (the stupidest girl in Whitby according to Mrs Medway, their cook of many years' standing) all busied themselves with preparation for the dinner to celebrate Mr Ashley's homecoming.

Constance had arranged flowers in all the vases, chandeliers were already lit, multi-faceted cut-glass drops twinkling as they picked up the glow from the fire, their polished prisms flashing a myriad showering sparks into the pair of glass mirrors across the room.

Polished silver shone. The two ornate candelabras with their scrolling branches were positioned at either end of the dining table, the cranberry epergne in the centre, its white flowers contrasting with its pink, trumpet-like vases and spun-glass baskets that hung from tall barley-sugar-twist walking sticks.

Silver cruets were filled, napkin rings clasped white starched linen, more logs were brought in for the fire and the fire-irons polished yet again.

While the dining room was overseen by Constance, Mrs Medway, issuing orders, reigned over the activities below stairs, further advising on the suitability of tureens and sauce boats, while adding the final touches to her sweet.

"Maria, the sauce—don't let it boil or it'll curdle!" And, not for the first time that evening, cook threw up her hands in despair, declaring that the meal would be ruined and they'd all be thrown into the street, and what would become of them then?

Maria swore inwardly and resolved yet again that when she was in a position of authority she would be much better-mannered than the Mrs Medways of this world: a thousand times more considerate than the turkey-necked woman who was now shouting abuse at her.

Then there was Ingrams, the butler, trying to look important in his fancy clothes, and pushing-in on the proceedings like a clucking hen, fussing over the bottles of wine and shouting at her whenever she so much as looked at them. "Don't touch!" he'd snap, "or you'll stir up the sediment."

For over an hour the wine had stood on the window ledge, next to the cut-glass jug with the silver mount. So jumpy he seemed, even when Mrs Medway went near it. One would think it was the first time he'd ever waited at table. Yet to hear him boasting of his days in Harrogate, a fine big house before his lordship died—and he, Ingrams, had been forced into obscurity and Whitby.

Well, just fancy.

For she knew that Mr High-and-mighty Ingrams could well have been in 'obscurity' for over twenty years, but also it was rumoured that he'd…

"Maria, you stupid girl! Look what you've gone and done now"—and the cook rushed forward to rescue another near-culinary disaster.

"Drat the girl," Mrs Medway fumed. "Would she never learn?"

While chaos reigned in the servant's quarters, upstairs in the library the master of the house sought sanctuary amongst his books. As he sipped his drink he once again thanked God for the safe return of his favourite son, Ashley.

The striking of the hour interrupted his silent prayer, and he slowly looked at the gold hunter he took from his waistcoat pocket, then at the library clock. The latter was slow by two minutes and, as he adjusted the hand accordingly, he stared absently as he'd done so many times at the maker's name on the brass dial: *Webster, Whitby*.

Clockmakers; boatbuilders; the alum works; the whaling industry; the two big banking houses in the town, Jonathan and Joseph Sanders; the establishment of Robert Campion—and one of the few woman bankers in the country, Margaret Campion. Add to these banking names that of Miles Wells & Co in Bridge Street, and in the old Market Place that of Clarke, Richardson and Hodgson.

Then there were chandlers, and the boatyards in the upper harbour where, at the turn of the century, the whaling ship *Experiment*, captained by Francis Agar, had been built. And two years later the *Aimwell*, built by Messrs Fishburn and Brodrick (the aforementioned captain being the owner of the vessel).

Also in Fishburn's Yard the *Cullandsgrove*, of six hundred and three tons, was built that same year, though their largest vessel, the *Esk*, of six hundred and twenty-nine tons and mounting forty-four guns, was built some twenty years previously.

More recent was Whitby's first lifeboat, built by Henry Greathead and stationed at the west side of the harbour, while hand-in-hand with the actual shipbuilding went Whitby rope-makers, sail-makers and the manufacture of sail cloth: the three principal makers being Chapman, near Spital Bridge, Impey's in the upper part of Bagdale and T& J Marwood of Flowergate, now producing over seven thousand yards weekly.

The busy quay, the Custom House, silversmiths, even clay pipe-maker, seamstresses, bonnet and stay makers, small shopkeepers, the fishing industry, the salting and curing of the aforementioned—the town was indeed becoming an important landmark in modern times, in addition to its past association with names such as the poet Cædmon, the abbess Hilda, and one must add to that the name of Capt James Cook. And perhaps, in the distant future that of Ashley Langden would be added to the roll of fame. His youngest, his favourite, son.

Stanhope, the eldest son, was a man-of-the-law, serious, and in these days inclined to stoutness through over-indulgence in food and wine. While in complete contrast his wife Sapphire, mother of their two sickly-looking children, had nothing to commend her as her jewel of a name might have suggested. For there was no sparkle. Indeed, her dowdy parson's-grey clothes and sallow flat face (and equally flat bosom) made her an altogether pitiable creature. She smelled of sickness and *sal-volatile*, was forever ailing and moaning with a whining voice befitting one having so many afflictions. How Stanhope could tolerate her was something his father had never been able to understand.

His second son, Westwood, had fared little better, having been foolish enough to imagine that marrying Beatrice Hardacre would permit him open access to the Hardacres' wealth. Beatrice, with her sharp blistering tongue and eyes that spat fire in opposite directions at the same time was enough to put off all but the very bravest of fortune hunters.

Her raucous voice made her little better than a fish-wife, for money does not buy breeding or good manners, and in her instance, both seemed sadly lacking. Their marriage-bed had produced a son who was fat and stupid. Fortunately for the Langden dynasty, their union had produced no further offspring.

How very different from his daughters-in-law was his own daughter, Constance, who possessed both brains and beauty. At twenty-three she could converse better than most men on political issues, was widely read, and had an ability to think for herself. Why—Constance seemed to know much more about the navy and the war against this damned Napoleon than did the very Admiralty!

She would peruse the *Leeds Intelligencer*, together with *The Times* newspaper, reading aloud accounts from one Admiral Millbanks on the state of the navy and any enemy ships captured. Perhaps this was on account of Lynton, the man she was soon to marry, being a surgeon on one of His Majesty's ships.

James was seized with a sudden fear that… but he strove to dismiss it and tried hard to concentrate on their two guests. These, because they'd grown up with the Langdens, seemed more like members of the family than simply "friends". Little was known of Tom and Leah's background, though James fancied that their parents had been gentlefolk: from somewhere near York he'd been led to believe. There had been a fire and...

But not wishing to dwell on such terrible matters, James focused his mind on the evening meal. A celebration of his son's safe return, and the opportunity for Ashley and Leah to announce their betrothal.

As the head of the Langden family sipped his Madeira, the other family members were putting the final touches to their evening attire.

Constance, hair piled high and held in place with combs and pins, wearing her newest gown with its high waist and provocative cleavage, posed before her mirror and carefully studied the effect. The emerald-green watered-silk clung to her curves while the diaphanous overskirt, with an open front to reveal the lavish beadwork, was an exact copy of the London fashion that Ashley had sent her earlier.

Tonight she strove to make herself look particularly attractive. But—and even she had to admit it—had she dressed in rags she would have appeared gracious and elegant in the company of her two sisters-in-law.

How she pitied Stanhope. The small-minded conversations he had to endure, day-on-day, year-on-year. Sapphire should by rights be the wife of some long-suffering country parson, instead of that of a successful lawyer. Why—Constance doubted that she had a decent dress to her name. And Beatrice, despite her family's wealth, was little better. Hair scraped back into a bun, a shiny red face and no table manners whatsoever. And what an awful squint. One never knew which way she was looking. Westwood had sold himself for money like some prize bull at a hiring fair. But Ashley had... but she put such thoughts from her mind, for the engagement had to remain a secret until it was announced at dinner.

Constance looked in her jewel box, and decided on the aquamarine and seed-pearl necklace. She had some earrings to match, and she'd wear her gold...

A sudden knock on the door made her start.

"Yes?"

"It's Ashley. May I come in?"

Her fingers smoothed the dress over her body before she called, "Yes, I'm nearly ready."

He stood in the doorway, blond curls falling over his forehead, his face wreathed in smiles.

"Well?"

"You all done-up for me?" Then in a brotherly way he teased her. "Or is this all for Tom Metcalfe's benefit? You bin seein' 'im in secret, wench?"

"Oh, beloved brother," and Constance took up a theatrical pose, "you have guessed our shame and cardinal sin—for I am betrothed to another."

"Wicked woman!"

"Methinks… that we shall have to run away together, and raise lots of children."

"Are you going to get married first?"

"Oh no," Constance giggled, "besides, I love Lynton."

"This is too much. Begone!"—and Ashley dramatically held out a hand pointing to the door.

"Oh Ashley"—and their play-acting over as quickly as it had begun, Constance threw her arms round him. "Oh, it's so very, *very* wonderful to have you home again. I know Papa's missed you, but not nearly so much as me. Life can be so… dreadfully boring. With you away, and Lynton at sea, and… well the house has been so quiet since mother died. It's very rare we have visitors, these days."

"But surely, Stanhope and Westwood— "

"Are boring too. And as for Sapphire and Beatrice… well, they're not like us. Do you remember when we were young and we decided to run away together? We reached Upgang Lane before they caught us."

"And I got a good hiding and was made to share the same bedroom as Westwood from then on."

"And then… there was the time we were going to stowaway on a ship and sail to America… and we tried to get Tom to come with us."

Ashley changed the subject. "Leah's very beautiful, isn't she? I suppose… while I've been at sea… she'll have had lots of young men all wanting to—"

"If you mean have any of them been proposing marriage, then—"

"They haven't, have they?"

"There's only one man I know of… and that's supposed to be a secret until it's announced this evening."

A grin spread across his face. "She's told you, then?"

"We're like sisters, we tell each other everything."

"And you approve?"

"Oh yes. For I was so afraid you might meet someone in London, say. Some society beauty who'd put us all to shame."

Then Constance took his hand and, perching on the edge of the bed, asked, "What's London really like? I remember reading somewhere that the London theatre was no more than 'a sobriquet for gilded immorality' with courtesans occupying front-line boxes at Covent Garden, using them merely as a shop window for displaying their bodies, and paying up to two hundred pounds a season."

Ashley stared wide-eyed, unable to decide whether or not to be shocked at his sister's choice of reading material. Then, face relaxing, he murmured, "I wish you'd told me earlier."

"Idiot."

"And there was me, wasting my time, going to places like Drury Lane to watch *Love Laughs at Locksmiths…* when I wasn't in the gambling houses."

Her eyes grew wide.

"It's very respectable, really," he explained. "After all, Ministers of the Crown are numbered among the members at Croxfords—even the Duke of Wellington's a member. Much worse are the London parks, where the professional ladies drive through in open carriages to display themselves. And at the Argyle Rooms, where membership is more exclusive than having one's name in Debrett, I was reliably informed of the annual ball for the Fashionable Impures, where, and I quote…"—and Ashley paused for effect—*"the seductive orbs of nature, undisguised, heaved like the ocean with circling swell."*

"Sounds absolutely disgraceful," Constance admonished him, yet delighted with this juicy tit-bit. "You've obviously been leading a life of complete and utter debauchery, and I feel that we should end this suggestive conversation here and now, nor must it be repeated to any others in the family, certainly not to Sapphire". Then she had an idea. "I say—shall we go to the theatre in Skate Lane tomorrow evening? We could ask Tom and Leah to accompany us."

"Mmm. If you like."

"And then you can point out all 'those women'."

"In Whitby? You're more likely to see the Press-Gang, as they cart away all the able-bodied young men."

Constance shook her head. "The theatre displays a notice saying quite clearly that the captain in-charge pledges his honour that no person whatever shall be impressed, or in any way molested by his party in Whitby, on the play night between the hours of five in the afternoon till eleven at night. And the play will be over by ten, so you and Tom will be quite safe."

"Then we'll risk it, if Tom agrees."

"Good. Now, fasten this necklace, and we'll—"

"In London," Ashley interrupted, "one sees exiled French aristocrats with their women daringly sporting a red velvet ribbon around their neck *a-la-Guillotine.*"

"Gruesome."—and Constance pulled a face.

"And even more terrible than that. For in London—and I'm not at all sure I should be telling you this, or that you'll understand what I'm about to disclose—but in the heart of London… there are 'Molly Houses'."

Her eyes grew wide as her brother explained as politely as he could, "where men… go to get to know other men."

"Like a club, do you mean?" she purposely teased, "where they meet in brotherly friendship and—?"

He ignored her pretended naivety as he continued, "And there's an abundance of smart military gentleman, even commissioned officers buying drinks for sailor boys… and… "

"Yes?"

"Taking them to the private rooms and facilities that are available and… er… well… you know."

"Oh, my dear brother, I am quite overcome by such startling revelations," and pretending to faint in his arms Constance suddenly asked, "what do these sailor boys charge—what's their *bottom price?*"

As the two fell about laughing, voices coming from downstairs told them that the first of the family dinner guests had arrived, and from the top of the stairs they could recognise the stentorian tones of their brother Stanhope. As the entered the drawing room he was stood in front of the hearth, papa seated in his favourite armchair.

"…Ashley!" the thunderous voice boomed out, halfway through a sentence.

"Welcome home"—and the half-hearted greeting he instinctively knew he'd get even before he saw her bob up from the gilded salon chair was from Sapphire. "How… well you look." And the scent of lavender sluggishly reached his nostrils as his sister-in-law stepped forward to plant a nervous, apologetic kiss on his cheek. Ashley wondered if his two nephews were unfortunate enough to take after their mother. He sincerely hoped not.

"And for how long this time, may we ask?"—and his brother was standing in front of him.

"Sorry…?"

"Before you find some new ship and go off on your travels? You'd do well to consider the whaling fleet—and Mr Scoresby. He's a more-than-fair man by all accounts, and they say he runs good ships."

Ashley paused, then casually replied, "I'm not in any real hurry."

"But if… when… you do decide," and Stanhope was not prepared to be fobbed off with half-answers, "I may be able to help you. The Scoresbys and I have done business on several occasions."

At that point Ingrams opened the door, coughed respectfully, then announced, "Mr and Miss Metcalfe."

"Show them in, Ingrams," and the host rose to welcome his guests. "Now we need only Westwood and Beatrice, then we can dine."

Ashley stared in pleasant wonderment at the girl wearing a similar style of dress to that of his sister, with deliciously tantalising blonde hair taken back and put in ringlets, at the blue eyes, the pretty little mouth. She was like a delicate porcelain shepherdess.

She was also wearing the betrothal necklace, and he thought yet again how wonderful it would be when they were married and… then from the corner of his eye he noticed Constance and made a supreme effort to control himself.

"Tom"—and Ashley took his hand. "So good to see you. Both of you."

"Hallo, Ashley."

"How's your uncle?"

Tom and Leah looked at one another and Tom replied for them both, "He still has his 'good' days occasionally."

"Have you brought any souvenirs back with you?" Sapphire timidly asked.

"Has he not!"—his sister replied for him. "Only a great big parrot."

"Oh, lovely!" And Leah clapped her hands in delight. "We must see him, mustn't we, Tom. Can he talk?"

"He swears," Ashley confessed.

The wheels of a carriage were heard outside the windows, heralding the arrival of Westwood and Beatrice. After announcing them, Ingrams again inspected the dining room, hurriedly exchanging two of the tall-stemmed glasses for another identical two.

The claret, earlier decanted, was standing on a silver salver in readiness, the rest of the wines arranged on the serving table. The candelabras were lit, another log placed on the fire and, after several anxious minutes below stairs, Ingrams announced that dinner was ready.

Throughout the meal Leah, enraptured, clung to Ashley's every word as he described his exploits. Not even the cross-eyed stare of his sister-in-law could distract him, or Constance's look of mock-disapproval on more than one occasion, and the homecoming celebration meal ended with lemon syllabub served with angels' trumpets.

When everyone had had their fill, Ashley and Leah's betrothal was officially announced. The ladies retired and the gentleman took to their port and cigars. Ashley, caring little to discuss the war or speculate on Napoleon's latest manoeuvres, and knowing absolutely nothing of the new alterations envisaged for the harbour, looked to Tom for a drinking partner.

Stanhope expounded on the harbour trade—and the harbourside whores—then recounted the uproar in the town just days before, when contraband had been seized and carried on carts to the Customs Warehouse in Sandgate, much to the annoyance of the townsfolk.

Ashley refilled his glass, and Tom's. He wished he could talk to Leah, for now that their forthcoming marriage had been made public there were things they had to discuss. While Tom, who'd have preferred to be alone with his friend instead of taking part in a family gathering, felt more than a trifle uncomfortable under Stanhope's constant glare.

The pompous, booming voice thundered on, punctuated at intervals by Westwood trying to add some sparkle to the conversation, but failing miserably in this. The two men did not notice when their brother and his friend disappeared. Talking to a macaw was, to Ashley and Tom, preferable by far to listening any longer to Stanhope Langden.

Ashley suddenly realised that if he were really to say goodbye to his seafaring days and put roots down on dry land, then it would need to be at the opposite end of Whitby from his elder brother.

Chapter 4

The cruel biting wind from the sea teased-out a thin line of distant cloud as the whaler *Sea Wolf*, in readiness for her imminent voyage, took on last-minute provisions, much to the excitement and interest of those watching, but to the consternation and squawking of the hens in their crudely fashioned sea-bound accommodation.

Reputed to be the bravest, most fearless of all seamen were the whalers. And in anticipation of a prosperous voyage, their spirits and hopes were as high as the ragged clouds being stretched across the horizon. The vessel, its seams freshly caulked, mast and spars oiled, sporting sails of new unblemished canvas, was being loaded with food and equipment. Potatoes, flour, tea, salted pork, quantities of ship's biscuits, lime juice, timber, spare canvas, ropes, various tools, casks of rum, ship's beer, candles, tobacco and other essentials.

The assembled crew of over thirty local men and boys had already hoisted the customary garland made up of sweethearts' and wives' ribbons, and had lashed it well above the deck to the top of the main mast as a symbol of good fortune. Each one of them was hoping that on the *Sea Wolf's* return their wages would be supplemented by a bonus in return for a ship full of whale oil, and other trophies besides.

Ashley saw the looks on their faces as he and Leah stood, hand-in-hand, watching the near-fever pitch activity, and for one moment Ashley envied them, until he turned to Leah. This was where his happiness lay, and he would never go back to sea.

Yet, he thought, never had a trade been so colourful, such a calling of contrasts—so cruel, barbaric and totally destructive of life. Yet if it were a prosperous expedition then it became rewarding and fulfilling.

Before heading for the whaling grounds proper, the *Sea Wolf* would first call at Orkney, and there sign-on more hands, probably the same number again. Then, heading for the open sea, a bloody massacre would begin of any living creature unfortunate enough to cross their path. The beluga, nicknamed the sea canary; the narwhal, known as the unicorn because of its single spiral tusk; the walrus; the seals off Newfoundland and Greenland; and, sadly, their defenceless young for their soft fur. And finally, on reaching their destination, the arctic fox and polar bear. Sometimes the bear would have with her a cub, which, after the mother had been slaughtered would be taken to the ship and brought home to England, to be sold to some travelling fair.

Often, not so valuable things were slain, neither for food or their pelts, but simply for sport. Guillemots, burgomaster gulls, snowy owls, even the albatross—for nothing was safe or sacred. The whaling fleets left a bloody trail of death and destruction; endless, indiscriminate massacre; even before reaching the whaling grounds. It was a pitiless and pitiful trade, entered into by desperate men in a last effort to save themselves and their families from starvation.

Threatened by sub-zero temperatures, shifting ice, hunger and disease and the frightening possibility that the ship would end up trapped in an icy grave and never return. Furthermore, as had been known, men so very near starvation would resort to cannibalism to survive.

On their eventual return (if they were fortunate enough to do so), now burned brown by the arctic sun, unshaven and emaciated, their clothes in tatters, they made a sorry sight. Yet their ship could be 'clean' with no trophies—nothing—except the men themselves. These, through sheer boredom, could well have gambled away the wages due to them.

Even a "prosperous" voyage could have an unfortunate ending, for there was ever the threat that, whilst only a few miles from shore, they'd be boarded by the press-gang. For whaling ships were a prime target, as those who sailed in them were considered ideal for withstanding the primitive conditions of His Majesty's Navy. Many a time all the able-bodied were dragged from the hold, manacled one to the other and forcibly removed.

Within the last twelve months, so he'd been reliably informed, the Whitby ship *The Wisk*, with Thomas Holt part-owner and his nephew Thomas Holt as master, had been boarded, and Robert Miller, the ship's carpenter had been impressed into the Navy while the ship was in London. Invariably ships' surgeons were taken, for there never were sufficient volunteers.

Ashley was again thankful he'd sailed the China Seas—and not with the Scoresbys' whaling ships. He looked again at Leah: his decision to stay on land had been a wise one. Mysterious, faraway places no longer lured him. His happiness was by his side.

She must have read his thoughts. "I'm glad you're not with them."

"You'd never catch me on a whaler."

"Or any other ship. You won't… will you, Ashley?"

They were interrupted by the noise of the bridge opening as the *Sea Wolf*, sailing on the full tide, moved out majestically. A spick-and-span ship: yet on her return she would be dirty and greasy, masts torn, riggings broken and needing repair, and invariably with less men than on the outward journey.

Still holding hands, Ashley and Leah cheered as did the other onlookers: the old hags who hung about the quay and lived off their wits; the beggar openly exhibiting scars and mutilations he claimed were the result of a whaling accident; barefoot children; two harbourside whores, looking dreadful in the light of day and other, more 'respectable', inhabitants of Whitby.

A group of women, shawled, some with tears in their eyes, waved goodbye to their loved ones. A woman there was, fat and toothless, whom Leah recognised as one of Tom's regular customers. Then Leah saw the woman from Tin Ghaut, who seemed to be forever giving birth to babies with ginger hair. Glancing at her ripe figure, Leah calculated there would be another ginger head appearing before the month was out. If her husband was on board the *Sea Wolf*, then things would be difficult for her.

Gulls screamed, men waved and the ship moved to the mouth of the harbour. A sudden gust of wind made Leah shudder, and she nestled closer to her companion. She could feel his strength, smell the freshly-laundered linen of his shirt and the sultry cologne he wore, and as they stood together the *Sea Wolf*, her sails now bellied and ballooning in the wind, moved toward the open sea.

Slowly the crowd of onlookers dispersed, and Ashley and Leah walked toward Bagdale to stand and stare once more at the property that was being offered for sale, and would hopefully be their new home.

"Isn't it lovely!" Leah enthused. "Oh Ashley, I do hope we're able to—"

"If you want it, then it's yours. We'll still have lots of money to live on, and I shall soon be working again."

"And… when we're married, I'll be such a good wife, I really will. I've always loved you, you know. I'll try so hard to make you happy."

"We must both of us… try to make each other happy," and Ashley again marvelled at his good fortune, as he stared at the imposing house with its long garden and elegant portico. "You'll need… a cook, a housekeeper, and a maid, or whatever you think… and perhaps—"

"But shall we be able to afford to pay wages to—"

"Have no fears," he was quick to assure her. "Whitby's a wealthy town and I shall have no shortage of patients who'll think nothing of paying ten… twenty guineas, simply for a consultation."

She stared in astonishment.

"And much more, if I have to treat them, or perform surgery. We're going to make lots of money… and when we're married we can have lots of babies."

Leah giggled. Ashley—and a splendid house—and babies besides! It all seemed too good to be true.

The following afternoon they made a proper tour of inspection, Ashley admiring the panelled hallway and stucco plasterwork while Leah approved of the drawing room with its seemingly huge windows, especially compared to the apothecary shop on Church Street where she'd grown up.

There were more reception rooms, with elaborate moulded ceilings and deep friezes, marble fireplaces, polished oak floors, a huge kitchen and butler's pantry, keeping-cellars, endless bedrooms and attics, and an impressive sweeping staircase.

The two of them moved from room to room, mentally furnishing each one with deep drapes to the windows, glittering chandeliers from the ceiling centrepieces, girandoles holding tall candles, gilded overmantles, a grand piano (for show, as neither of them could play such an instrument)—even a harp. And a *very* elaborate and commodious cage for the macaw, which by now they'd christened Elijah.

Chapter 5

Spring gave way to summer, then that season to autumn, and Ashley, anxious to make a name for himself, acquired his first patients.

More than once had he been called by the recruiting officer to examine the latest haul of impressed men to declare them fit for the Navy. Providing they were not obviously idiots, deformed or minus a limb they were passed as suitable, which seemed to him a much safer proposition than the fate awaiting him with a comparative newcomer to the town: a Mrs Dalgleish who, it was rumoured, was openly running a house of ill-repute in what passed as a respectable part of Whitby.

It was very early in the morning when Ashley glanced surreptitiously up and down the street before knocking on the door. It was opened by someone no longer a boy, but not quite a man, dressed in a pale green watered-silk waistcoat over a white shirt over his black skin. He had billowing sleeves, and lace at his neck and wrists, which contrasted sharply with his black tight knee-breeches and stockings. There were silver buckles on his shoes, the whole ensemble being topped by a powdered wig tied with a black ribbon. A world away from the negroes skulking around the quay when foreign ships came into port: this was more like a prince.

"Mrs Dalgleish is expecting you"—and Ashley was ushered into a hallway which sported a huge mirror in an elaborately carved gilded frame above a similarly opulent side-table on which (in an effort perhaps to give the place 'respectability') rested a bible.

The young man offered a silver salver to Ashley for his visiting card, made a slight bow as he took two paces back then, holding himself erect, the salver held aloft as though it were some trophy, he moved down the hallway. He gave two knocks on a door before opening it, then gave a discreet cough before seconds later re-appearing and announcing, "Mr Langden, Mrs Dalgleish will see you now. If you will be so kind as follow me, Sir."

The room was lavishly furnished with heavy velvet drapes to the windows, before which stood a harpsichord with a shepherd and shepherdess painted under the wing. There was a credenza with ormolu mounts and porcelain panels, and a *bonne-de-jour* inlaid with garlands of flowers in various coloured woods. Above the marble fireplace was a portrait of a young woman, and across the room another painting of cupids, quite unashamed in their nakedness... and from a gilded settee a figure dressed in pale blue silk rose up to greet him.

"Mr Langden, how very kind of you to call. Now, before our business, may we offer you some refreshment? Xavier, wine for our guest." And the young man nodded, then withdrew. "I always think part of being a good hostess is to have a well-stocked wine cellar, wouldn't you agree?"

"I... er..."

"But to partake of my mulberry wine was not the reason for inviting you. No, it is in a purely professional capacity."

"Then, you are ill, perhaps, and wish me..."

"Heavens, no, it's that I need you..."

But at that point she was interrupted by the re-appearance of her young serving-boy, offering glasses of deep ruby nectar. Ashley sipped, then suddenly choked on his drink as the voice continued, "...to give me certificates declaring that my charges are free of the venereal pox."

Ashley took deep breaths to compose himself, before explaining "I'm first and foremost a surgeon, Madam, not a physician. Therefore any document signed by me would be quite worthless."

"But I always had a surgeon examine my girls in London, where I ran a house in Covent Garden," Mrs Dalgleish insisted. "I paid him ten guineas for each one, every time I had recourse for my girls to avail themselves of his services."

Ashley echoed the sum, momentarily tempted.

"London seems a very different place to this part of Yorkshire"—and she gave a sigh. "But, with the threat of royal scandals looming, and—and it is always the woman who pays, you know, the men get away scot-free—it was 'suggested' that a temporary move would be... appropriate. Two of my girls are with me, and there's also Amy. But Amy is for marriage, not for pleasure."

Ashley drank deeply as the procuress continued. "When I was young and in residence, Mr Langden, I entertained the famous... and the infamous. I was even painted by Sir Joshua—and not simply as a background model, but a portraiture subject. Most of my profession will be forgotten, but I have been immortalised on canvas. My beauty will live on."

"Indeed!"

Fingers adorned with diamonds and sapphires reached for a gold box containing visiting cards. "Take one with you, Sir," the painted procuress urged, and Ashley read the words: *Bernice and Camille, well-coached in the art of pleasing gentlemen of quality. Special consideration given to inexperienced young men, or those of the cloth.*

"Heavens. Is that the time? Then I must be away, for I have other calls to make."

"But Camille was so looking forward to being of service to you—without any payment, of course. Gentlemen tell me she is irresistible, for she is well-coached, and quite prepared to accommodate any gentleman's 'unusual' tastes.

"Bernice, slightly younger, is slim and equally accommodating… and, Mr Langden, they do so miss London society. As for Amy? Well, truth to tell, she's not been with me long. But my establishment was so highly recommended that I felt it my duty to secure her future as best I could.

"She was seen last season in my carriage as we rode through the London park, and also at the opera, and has attracted much interest. But she is untouched, and is for marriage before pleasure. There have been tentative proposals from an Earl, and also a very influential Member of Parliament… and by the end of the year, who can tell?

"Although still pure and untouched she is being coached by Camille on how to please men, and Xavier—well, the brave boy helps with the role-play… provided there is no penetration. To command a high price, she must remain a virgin."

Ashley drained his glass, his head spinning. The liquor was powerful, and he stared again past gilded cherubs and naked statues at a woman still beautiful, despite her age and profession.

Then he realised that the negro servant had suddenly reappeared… and with him a very scantily dressed young woman, who was suggestively running her hands over her curvaceous body.

She turned toward him—and Ashley made a bolt for the door.

As he hurried through the town he decided that that would be the last time he would call on Mrs Dalgleish. Yet he had to smile when he imagined the look on Stanhope's face should it ever become known he'd been seen running from the local brothel.

Such a busy man his brother seemed, while he'd become very much a man of leisure. But, he told himself, when he and Leah were husband and wife, and settled in their new home, then he'd be able to use this as his business address and consulting room. "When we are married" was how Leah began most sentences when the two of them were alone together. Why—she was beginning to sound like his sister Constance, with her grand plans for when she became Mrs Lynton Shaw. Yet it was so rare that she and Lynton were able to see each other, and most of their contact was through letter writing.

There had been a brief spell earlier in the year, when his ship had been in Plymouth, when Constance had boarded the coach to York, then took a series of overland coaches to meet up with him. Their time spent together had been short, for they had also called to see his parents. On her return she seemed subdued, for they had not been able to set a date for their marriage due to his 'commitments'. Once again Ashley reflected on how lucky he was to be able to see Leah every day.

His next port-of-call was Church Street, where he would keep her company while Tom was away collecting the various herbs and roots he needed to prepare cough syrups for winter. The sun's lazy fingers were already streaking the sky and the early morning mist had disappeared. As, he imagined, the apothecary would have done by now.

Chapter 6

As horse and rider left Whitby and climbed the coastal road to take them further up the coast, Tom Metcalfe looked out over the sea.

From this vantage point the morning sun spilled over the water like liquid gold from a crucible. The air was shimmering, such was the fine autumn morning. And what Tom had earlier regarded as a drudgery was already becoming a pleasant diversion from his usual day's work.

A sudden unexplained illness afflicting Walter meant that Tom now had to search the hedgerows himself to find the wherewithal to concoct his medicines and the like. For days the old man had been complaining about stomach pains and had finally, much to his daughter's consternation, taken to his bed saying he was about to die.

He'd even lost his craving for the mushrooms he'd been devouring in great quantities. Yet when Tom saw these fungi he was able straightaway to diagnose the old man's malady. He'd been slowly killing himself, for although his knowledge of herbs and roots was reliable, on poisonous and hallucinatory mushrooms he was less of an authority.

As Tom picked his way along the ruttle road he recognised a familiar figure coming toward him. A striding gait and frame as lean as fiddle strings, there was no mistaking Malahide O'Connor, the Preventative Officer for this particular stretch of coastline.

"Top o' the mornin'," the Irishman greeted him.

"And to you, O'Connor."

He was a man who appeared where one least expected him, which was perhaps something to do with the job, yet it was indeed rare that O'Connor brought smugglers or contraband goods to the attention of the Custom House officials.

His was an easy life, and O'Connor had often boasted that he infinitely preferred being born lucky to being born rich. For a man was so easily tempted to squander or gamble away his wealth—whereas Lady Luck would be with him till his dying day.

Tom continued his journey, sometimes riding, sometimes leading the horse. Midday found him outside an inn, and upon entering the low-raftered tavern he was greeted by the landlord and also by two men sucking on clay pipes. The wisps of tobacco lazily drifted upwards, mingling with the applewood smoke from the fire and the smell of home-brewed ale.

As Tom raised his tankard and eagerly quenched his thirst the older man leisurely, and with practised skill, spat into the flames. Then, before returning the pipe to his lips stated, "You'll be new to these parts." It was not a question but a declaration and, not waiting for confirmation, he picked up the fire iron and trailed its point over the spittle hissing on the coals.

Tom drank again. "Aye."

The man deliberated. Then turning to his companion, whose coat was frayed at the cuffs, explained, "The gentleman'll be on important business, Caleb, or why else would he venture into these parts?"

His companion looked at Tom carefully. Then, as though it were a supreme effort, slowly nodded in agreement.

Wiping his mouth with the back of his hand, Tom replied, "I do assure you, gentleman, my being here is quite innocent. Nor is it of any secret nature. I'm an apothecary by trade, and I'm here to gather herbs and roots such as I require in the making of my remedies. I'm from Whitby town, where I'm in business on my own account. I'm hoping to travel as far as the corn-mill that separates the parishes of Hinderwell and Easington.

"Then likely as not... you'll be goin' near Steeas?" Frayed-cuffs spoke in rough country dialect.

Tom seemed uncertain. "Aye? Would this be—?"

"Steeas." Frayed-cuffs repeated the word.

"A fishing village some miles further up the coast," the old man explained, staring into the depths of his tankard, "and you'd do best to give it a wide berth. They can be... unfriendly... in Steeas."

There followed an awkward silence—a charged one—as the two seated figures looked at one another. Then one of them nodded toward a glowing piece of coal that had fallen from the fire-grate and was now smouldering on the hearth.

Tom sensed a dark foreboding, and a malevolence in their manner as, like prophets of doom, the two of them fixed their stare on the nearly extinguished ember. Tom, suddenly uneasy in the company of Frayed Cuffs and his friend, finished his ale, then muttered, "I'll bid you good day, gentlemen, for I've things to attend to."

They seemed not to hear, or if they did, they took no notice. He swung himself into the saddle and rode off into the afternoon sun.

Soon the next hamlet came into view. As he passed the church a man with a flock of sheep filled the road, and from the nearby smithy came the clink of metal struck. As Tom drew nearer he saw the giant figure of the blacksmith holding in long tongs the white-hot horseshoe he was fashioning, There were heavy but precise blows from a hammer, a shower of sparks, then the metal was buried again in the heat of the forge.

Tom let the mare casually pick her way along the pot-holed road, and when this finally petered out he took the coastal path along the cliff tops. Tom tried to recognise the first of the landmarks his usual herb-collector had mentioned.

Somewhere along the cliffs was an ironstone mine which, he was assured, he would have no difficulty in recognising. Perhaps, he told himself, it would be just beyond the field of harvesters now coming into view. He stopped and listened to the swish of scythes, gazing toward the women hard at work. With their billowing aprons and cloths tied round their heads they reminded him of cranberry pickers he'd once seen on the moors near Pickering.

The autumn sun kissed his arms and the nape of his neck, the breeze from the sea was welcoming—and suddenly in the distance he saw the mine. Higher up the coast, he'd earlier been informed, were alum workings—and between these two landmarks: *Steeas!*

He crossed a field, rough with stubble, now a feasting ground for pheasants sporting green and imperial purple. The gulls were circling, screaming, and suddenly he looked down and caught his first sight of the cluttered roof tops.

The houses were seemingly built on top of each other, or prised between, and fell tumbling down to the sea. As he came nearer, dogs barked and children in rags gawped as he began to descend the steep gully. Beyond the houses was the sea. While much nearer, from dirty window panes, more than one face stared as he made his way down the rough path.

A woman, as old again as time and dressed entirely in black, save for her unwashed bonnet (which he took to be mauve) stood motionless, surveying him, her ample frame filling her doorway.

The houses were now beginning to alter in appearance. There was a well-proportioned property to his right, with broad steps and iron railings, and he assumed it to be perhaps the home of some ship owner, or even a retired sea captain. The next house had a flight of stone steps running along the front of the building, leading, he presumed to the owner's living accommodation, while the underneath would probably house lobster-pots, or even domestic animals.

The afternoon was becoming unreal, as though he were in a dream. For there was something about this isolated fishing village. He could retrace his steps, he knew. But, as though led by some mysterious inner force, he had to continue, despite feeling vulnerable and very exposed.

The path wound on its sinuous way, then suddenly opened upon a cobbled square. Over railings, drying in the afternoon sun, were draped fishing nets, glistening with fish scales, and smelling of the same. Gulls screamed as they swooped toward the jutting cliff.

Then, for the first time, he noticed black birds—crow-like, were it not for their grey hoods—preening and cavorting themselves and squabbling over scraps of food. Undecided, and for some inexplicable reason, he stood watching their antics.

Then from one of the numerous alleyways a woman appeared and stepped into the sunlight. On seeing him, she straightaway pulled back, only to reappear. Seeming suddenly bold, she made her way toward the village well.

She was wearing a simple dark dress, hair tied back, her arms and shoulders brown from the elements. She was perhaps a few years older than Leah, and although lacking Leah's beauty, there was about her a simple yet hypnotic fascination.

For a long time Tom just stared, without then realising just how thirsty the journey had made him. He saw water splashing from the leather pitcher. He swallowed, then feeling bold himself he moved toward her.

Her head was bent forward and so she saw at first his shadow. Then, the rest of her quite still, she slowly turned and her face met his. Immediately he was under the spell of her deep searching eyes, dark and sorrowful—he knew not if it were but seconds or an era.

Then, suddenly realising how foolish he must be appearing, he said simply, "May I have a drink?"

As she offered the pail, Tom cupped his hands, then plunged them into the water. He drank long and greedily, not daring—not having the slightest inclination—to take his eyes off her.

"It's a... fine day," he managed, between gulps.

She nodded.

"The birds...?" Tom enquired as the more daring ones began to alight and hop around them. "Are they...?"

"Jackdaws—for this is Jackdaw Well."

Her voice was soft, and as she spoke one of the birds came very near to alighting on her arm. She wore plain golden ear-rings, and Tom had a sudden desire to see her in one of Leah's dresses—or the scarlet watered-silk that Constance filled so well. Finally he asked, in a voice that was strange to himself, "Is there... no one about in the village?"

"The men are fishing."

He paused, hopefully. Staring. Waiting for an invitation to Paradise. But her reply was crushing as she advised him, "you'd best be about your business—for they don't take kindly to strangers."

"They...?"

"The men of Steeas."

"But you said they were fishing."

"Aye—and they'll be in on the tide." And she turned to walk away, as the jackdaws circled in the air.

"I'm seeking the corn mill which lies on the two parish boundaries," Tom explained, then added, "Which way should I go?"

"Back the way you came. If you ride through the village and over the bridge, the older men and women will see you and you could be stoned, or worse. Go back the way you came, and take the track that leads around the village. The mill's some way inland."

"Thanks." Then as he was moving off himself he called to her, "My name's Tom. What is yours?"

"Sarah."

"Then I'd best… find the mill—then head for home."

Halfway up the steep climb he turned to look behind. She was watching him. Strange encounter, he thought. Strange woman.

Still, at least she'd given him directions… and even stranger advice. Walter Grainger had given no such warnings regarding the inhabitants of the fishing village, and as he looked back on thick treacly fumes emerging from every chimney-pot he likened it to staring into Hades.

Upon reaching the mill, the woman was still on his mind as he began (without giving it any real thought) to prise the plant roots from the rain-parched soil. Dried in fine sand they would become the main ingredient for his winter cough linctus. There was also some late-flowering yarrow, and honeysuckle that could be incorporated into candy.

The air was still. His nostrils detected the sweetness of apples being pressed, as did the drowsy wasps hovering near the mill's out-building. The autumn sun had lightened the sedge on either side of the mill race to a tawny gold, the reeds turning to rust, the wind-ruffled water with its palisade of rushes giving sanctuary to a flock of moor-hens.

Tom drew level with the parapet of the bridge that separated the two parishes when he saw, through the overhanging branches of a copper-beech, the figure of a woman. And straightaway he knew—he just *knew*—that it was Sarah.

As he came closer she slowly circled the clump of silver birch, then beckoned him to follow. Without a second thought Tom tethered his horse, then headed toward the delicate tracery of trees.

The bracken crackled underfoot as he picked his way through the salebrous undergrowth, and more than once he thought he'd lost her. And he'd stare around in near-panic only to be reassured by a flash of paisley-patterned shawl as he was being led further into the dense wood.

On reaching a sudden clearing he stopped, undecided as to which way he should proceed. Then he saw her come from behind a giant oak and, like a man bewitched, he hastened toward her.

Her voice was gentle. "Tom?"

"Aye—an' what's to do, then?" and he took her in his arms and began caressing her, and in a faraway voice, hitherto unknown even to himself, he asked, "Are we safe 'ere?"

For reassurance her fingers began undoing the fall-front of his breeches. As though in a trance, and putting up not the slightest resistance, Tom succumbed to her advances and willingly allowed himself to be seduced by this earth-goddess. Aroused by her soft, purring sounds and the sensuous fluttering of her hands over the most sensitive, secret parts of his anatomy, beneath a canopy of wavering lights and shadows from the giant oak, he was powerless to resist her advances.

He frantically lifted her skirts, and his bare buttocks began rising rhythmically as he pushed harder. He heard a moan that turned into a scream before her teeth sank into his lip, her body arched, fingers grabbed his hair.

Then the scream became a whimper of satisfied pleasure as they lay gasping, their lust temporarily sated. He could feel a trickle of sweat running from his hair as a voice, little more than a whisper was asking, "Was it all right, Tom? Did I please you?"

He stared into the liquid depths of her dark eyes, then at the open bodice, and by way of answer caressed the exposed breast. He kissed, then his tongue teased her dusky nipple before he murmured, "Oh aye, Sarah—you pleased me."

Then there was a stillness, and for a long time they lay at peace in one another's arms, till Tom casually took her hand and accidentally felt the ring on her finger.

The magic vanished. "Sarah, are you—?"

"He's at sea. 'Has been so for many a month. He disappeared, late one night."

"The press-gang?"

She shook her head, neither did she offer any further explanation.

And now that a cloud had come between them they must get dressed. Furtively, for they were no longer in the Garden of Eden. Sarah tugged at her skirt, then said simply, "I must get back before I'm missed."

"But I thought—"

"Yes, but there are others."

"Well..." Tom ventured lamely, "shall I see you again?"

"No—we'd best not." Her reply was like a drench of cold water.

"But… I thought what we did just now *meant* something to you. Though I don't live in these parts, I could always come into Steeas… if…"

She shook her head. "No good could come of it, believe me." The earlier sadness had returned to her eyes, as she managed to say, "It's best we go our separate ways."

"Then"—and Tom picked up his jacket and gave it a good shaking to dislodge the bracken—"I'd best be away, for I've a fair distance to travel."

She stood watching him, nodding in agreement.

"Shall we… kiss goodbye…?"—and Tom suddenly had his arms around her. She hung on to him, reluctant to release the only happiness, albeit fleeting, she had ever known.

"'Bye, Tom," she whispered. "'Bye, love."

Instead of muttering something incoherent, Tom suddenly felt bold and said, "Meet me again: day after tomorrow. Here—in the afternoon."

"No. I can't."

"Just by this oak," Tom called after her as she took leave of him. "I'll wait for you, Sarah." Then he went searching for Bess, whom he found contentedly munching the grass. He took one last look behind him. His earth-goddess had been spirited away.

Chapter 7

From his vantage point up on the hill near St Mary's, Tom looked down on a steaming cauldron of ships' masts and riggings. The horizon and skyline were quite indistinguishable from one another.

There was a warm stillness in the air, even the gulls were silent, the grass beneath his feet wet with autumn dew, the haulm of the hemlock draped in gossamer-like spiders' webs. But the hour was early, the morning sun would burn off the mist and the town would appear bright and polished, there'd be another new day and...

And as he began to descend the hundred-and-ninety-nine steps (he'd counted them so very many times) his thoughts again turned to his encounter the previous afternoon.

Impossible to describe—not that he dared, not even to Ashley.

Totally unexpected, to meet this complete stranger, and—could he really say, "make love to her"? Didn't you have to *know* someone first before you could love them? Yet neither could he debase their behaviour by thinking of it as nothing more than an act of copulation.

He could still see her eyes, run his fingers through her hair, feel the warmth of her body. Everything about the afternoon had been... just amazing.

Oh, he'd often heard men describe *that*—boasting about their own virility and prowess, and he'd had to pretend to understand, but it had never happened to him. For Sarah was the first woman he'd ever... made love to. And he had to call it that, because that was what it was. No—he didn't feel any more of a man that he did before it had happened. It just...

Oh, he was making all too much of it. Much better simply to forget the whole incident and concentrate on his daily chores. Seeing-to uncle; tying the herbs in neat bunches before hanging them to dry; keeping the woody roots of nightshade safely out of harm's way, also the starch-wort which was destined to become a cure for various maladies.

And—he had to consider this seriously—what would he do for help with uncle and the shop when Leah and Ashley were wed? Attending to customers would be the last thing on her mind. Nor did he imagine Ashley would agree to her spending her days in the shop when she had a fine house to oversee and, in the fullness of time, a young family to care for.

Perhaps he should think about... an apprentice? His uncle Nathan had taught him, and in turn he could pass on his knowledge to some willing young lad, and he might even—and he suddenly jumped the last couple of steps. Then he hesitated—undecided as to take a left turn into Church Street, or to turn to his right and meander along Henrietta Street and then to…

But he took the left turn. Work was beckoning.

The cobbles were shiny, the sun trying to break through. A fellow shopkeeper nodded to him. The street was coming to life, the residents of the town going about their daily chores.

On his right the Town Hall came into view. The original building, having suffered the ravages of time, had been rebuilt several years previously by Nathaniel Cholmley, a descendent of Sir William, who around 1650 was responsible for this landmark.

Supported on each side by handsome pillars, and surmounted by a rectangular clock turret topped by an octagonal domed bell cote and a clock, the Town Hall was where the manorial courts were held, and it also served as a toll-booth for the fairs coming to the town and traders attending the markets.

There was also the Court Leet held annually after Michaelmas, usually concerned with settling boundary disputes or punishing petty misdemeanours. The Court of Pleas was held every third Monday for the recovery of small debts. And, as occasion demanded, a Court of Pie-powder, held to settle any disputes that might arise when fairs were in the town. Whitby matters, very sensibly, were all settled in Whitby without outside "interference".

Nor was this the only fine building in Whitby, for there was, among others, the Tudor Manor House in Bagdale which, Tom imagined, was one of the oldest buildings in the town, and the Custom House in Sandgate, while on the outskirts of town and higher up the coast was Mulgrave Castle, the present building being a castellated mansion ordered by Lady Catherine Darnley, Duchess of Buckingham, the illegitimate daughter of James II, when she was the wife of John Sheffield, 1st Duke of Buckingham and Normanby.

He allowed himself a moment's secret boasting—he'd been a very clever pupil and his uncle had taught him much about Whitby.

Just minutes away from his own business premises, Tom quickened his pace, the morning getting brighter and sunnier by the minute. Alum-workers, carrying the marks of their trade on their faces from the previous day (he doubted that some of them ever washed), were darting into their workplace. The *White Horse and Griffin* was having barrels of beer delivered, the ever-present gulls were screaming and wheeling, and Sarah—oh no…! He had the shop to open. Thoughts regarding Sarah would have to keep.

From her upstairs window, Sarah Dacre gazed beyond flat scaurs of rocks to where white waves were breaking and gradually stealing the shore. Reluctant to begin her chores, she turned her back on the accumulated pile of clothes needing darning or patching, again staring out to sea.

She sensed from his manner that Tom, when he grew tired of waiting for her, as he must be by now, would come into the village to seek her out. She was trying to convince herself that while she was in this tiny attic bedroom she was "safe". Also she was away from the rest of the Dacre household—and the drudgery that was destroying her, day by day.

A bad morning's work it had been when, some five summers gone, she and her father as a last desperate measure presented themselves at the Hiring Fair, hoping to find work together on some farm. When fate had taken a hand—and things had ended up very differently.

She cringed when she thought of that day, when she'd felt two pairs of men's eyes on her. Acutely embarrassed, she'd stared down at wilting daisies trampled underfoot and hoped the men would go away. Then suddenly she caught her breath as she saw the older of the two men in conversation with her father, then leading him to the tent selling home-brewed beer, while the younger man was still loitering near.

"'Ere, what's up? 'Cat got your tongue?"

She gave him a haughty look. "What do you want?"

"What's yer name then, me beauty?"

"I didn't say. And I'm certainly not 'your beauty'."

"Well then," and the young man expertly spat, just missing his boots, "I'm askin' now, my fine lady."

"Sarah. Sarah Gibbons. My father, Wilf Gibbons, is a farm labourer. For the past two years since my mother died—God rest her soul—we've been working for a yeoman farmer the other side of Yarm. But a few months ago he died and the farm's been sold. So that's why we're reduced to seeking work in this manner.

"My dad's a harvester and as such carries papers declaring himself free of impressment. They've been signed and are all in order…" She spoke in a proud voice but, because she was now roused, suddenly forgot her vocabulary. "'Ee's still strong, and can do the work of any younger man hereabouts, and a good sight more than most, 'cos 'ee's nooan afraid o' 'ard work!"

"Well, you'm got spirit, if nowt else"—and as he spoke, a man and woman who'd been staring at her for some time came towards her.

"You seeking a position, dearie? Can you cook?"

"Yes, and sew," Sarah replied, "besides helping out with farm work if need be. But I'm here with my father. We must secure employment together in the same household."

The woman shook her head. "Nay, it's a lass as I need, to take t' load off me 'ands. We've more na enough farm 'ands."

"Any road, she's 'ired!"

"But there must be some mistake…"

"What d'yer think my old man an' yours is drinkin' together for? It's to seal the bargain."

Suddenly, the morning's events took on a new turn, as an horrific scenario began to unfold. Working for this father and son would be… and her breath became laboured, the world suddenly spinning. A hawker selling nick-nacks from a tray came by, and Sarah tried to run between him and the young man.

"Not so fast"—and he made a grab at her arm, "besides, where d'yer think yer off to?"

"Tell—tell my father—" and for the first time Sarah noticed the man's right hand: it was one big purple stain, even to the tips of the fingers.

The purple talons grabbed her. "You're stayin' 'ere, me beauty."

When the older man and her father returned, the worse for drink, the full horror of the morning started to unfold.

Later that day the nightmare began in earnest, as she left with the two strangers to take up her position as housekeeper and dogsbody for Isaac Dacre and his four sons, following the death of the wife and mother.

For the most part of the journey she had to walk, stopping only when the two men relieved themselves unconcernedly in full view of her. That evening, in a filthy cottage smelling of rotting fish and excrement, her life in Staithes began.

The next morning commenced with a strident banging on the front door and Isaac Dacre was confronted by an old crone garbed entirely in black, save for the heavy gold ear-rings which made the pierced holes into slits.

"Shame on thee an' thine," she spat out the words through the gaps in her teeth, "fer tha's nooan t' sense tha wor born wi', bringin' a foreigner ter Steeas. It'll bring yer nowt but bad luck, an' I'll bid thee good mornin'"—and the prophetess of doom, her mission completed, drew her cloak around her shoulders and like a giant crow hopped down the stone steps without a backward glance. Lydia Dacre, the matriarch of the family, had said her piece—and time would prove her right.

"Tha's gooan an' done it, nah," his brother Aaron teased, having to move swiftly to dodge Cain's fist. "Upset aunt Lydia, an' tha'll be out o' 'will."

"Upset *me*, either on yer, this mornin' an' yer'll be out o' that door reight quick. Nah, frame yersens, there's work ter do." As Isaac Dacre stirred and bullied his sons to begin their day's work, the household chores began for their new "housekeeper", which became the daily ritual.

Besides hungry mouths to feed there was the cottage to keep clean, dirty clothes to wash, muck to clear out brought in from their sea-boots and fishing tackle. For like the rest of the village the Dacres relied on the sea for a living, hence the eternal smell of fish that permeated the house.

She had also new tasks to learn. Fish to gut, herrings to salt, crabs and lobsters to boil, and as high summer approached she had to contend with the horrible stench of rotting fish-innards that hung over the village. Gulls feasted and grew fat and the jackdaws became almost tame—as did the flies that hovered over dung-heaps in tiny claustrophobic yards.

Sarah counted the days to the end of her twelve months, though Isaac Dacre, pleased at the strong pair of hands, saw no sense in relinquishing her, or indeed, having to pay another year's wages to her father if he could keep that help for nothing.

Cain, somewhat taken aback, stared at his father, hoping he would elaborate on his sudden suggestion.

"You'll... *wed* 'er?"

"Not me, gurt simpleton. Thee!"

"Nay, but I'm promised ter me cousin Zilpha."

"Tha'll do as I say. Tha nooan reight bright, Cain, when it cooms ter—"

"Cousins allus wed in Steeas, it keeps brass in 'family," Cain Dacre argued, "an' mi cousin can sooin' be knocked into shape. This Sarah's a quare 'un. Mind o' 'er own."

" 'Course, if tha nooan ready—couldn't *satisfy* a wife—then ah mun think abaht Aaron weddin' an' beddin' 'er."

"Ah'm twice the man me brother'll ever be!" The eldest son rose to the bait, forever jealous of his father's favourite, "but why—?"

"Because... because... well, a farmer changes 'bull every year to keep 'line 'ealthy, an' that's what we Dacres need ter do. We dooant want another simpleton in t' family—one's enough."

"Aye," his son agreed. He thought of Daniel, the youngest of the Dacres and little better than an idiot. Only weeks previously, unknown to his father, he had caused great amusement to his brothers after being dared into servicing some mongrel bitch that was on-heat. They now awaited the arrival of a litter of cross-breeds, half-canine, half-idiot. A smile crossed Cain Dacre's face at the thought—and his father took this for a sign of acceptance.

"Then it's settled?"

"Supposin' she don't agree? Or do we need to 'ave words wi' Wilf Gibbons? 'Ee could already 'ave made plans fer 'er—"

"'Ee'll nooan raise objections." His father sounded confidant. "'Ee wants 'off 'is 'ands, fer 'ee's gooan an' wedded a rich widder woman in Sleights. Owns several farms. 'Ee's done well."

When the plans were announced, Lydia Dacre put in yet another appearance. "Damn thee an' thee brood, Isaac Dacre, fer if that lad o' thine weds this foreigner, tha'll bring shame on us all."

"It's ter bring sanity back. All this interbreedin' an' incest—it's turnin' Dacres funny. Look at young Daniel, daft as a cabbage."

"Tak's after thee!"

"After 'is aunt Lydia, more na likely," he called after her, determined to have the last word. He would have done better though to keep his peace with her. For she had no issue of her own to leave her "brass" to, just nephews and nieces, and he hoped his own sons in the not-too-distant future would benefit from her bounty.

When the dreadful day arrived, carrying a prayer book, her mind far away and as though it were all a game, Sarah, at nearby Hinderwell church, took her wedding vows—and she and Cain were pronounced husband and wife.

She tried to remember the village weddings she'd known as a child, with the marriage wain piled high with gifts from the bride's parents being proudly pulled through the village by big shire horses, the gaily decorated cart loaded down with furniture, linens, pots and pans.

She could also recall the games she and other children in the village had played—"weddings" was a favourite. But there was always *something* lurking in the background: the thought that perhaps this was a real wedding. You were marrying this farmer's lad who was playing the bridegroom—it was actually happening, and your friends were chasing one another, playing games, and you and the bridegroom had to kiss, and promise to have lots of babies and...

And suddenly reality struck!

For this "wedding" *was* the real thing—she was now the wife of Cain Dacre. She looked at him, then at her father, already the worse for drink, and she wanted to run away. She wanted the day to begin again, and she *could* have run away—far, far away—from the nightmare she was now part of. And there was worse to come, as she spent the night huddled in the corner of a huge four-poster bed, terrified that at any moment her husband would come staggering in and demand his conjugal rights.

But in that she was safe—for the present. For months after her wedding, she remained a virgin, for Cain, clumsy and inexperienced, was totally unable to penetrate her, and sought solace in his ale and the companionship of his drinking cronies.

"Is there ter be a bairn on 'way sooin?" one of the men teased.

"'Appen it's a Barley Bairn," someone else started to bait him. "Wor it on 'way afore tha gat wed, Cain?"

"Shut yer bloody mouth." Cain's fist smashed into the man's nose and a brawl broke out—another brawl—and Cain arrived home with a split lip and an eye that looked like it had been turned inside out. Sarah was roughly pushed aside when she dared to ask what had happened.

"See this?" Her husband pointed to his mulberry eye. "One more word an' tha'll get one ter match."

It was not until the following summer, the village heavy with the smell of fish and privvies, that Sarah began to feel sick in the mornings. And the women, chattering among themselves, noticed a roundness in her figure, and what one of them whimsically described as a "yonderly look".

"Shu'll be 'avin' a bairn afore 'year end," the fat woman from Boathouse Yard predicted. Being herself a mother of eight she could speak with authority as she stood, arms akimbo, by Jackdaw Well. "Reckon as shu'll nooan be so stand-offish then."

"Oh aye," the near-toothless old bundle of rags standing next to her egged her on, "an' Lord knows, what a skrikin' there'll be when shu starts. Awful, 'avin yer first bairn. An' owd Lizzie does nowt ter 'elp these days. Midwife? Huh, shu couldn't deliver two penn'oth o' 'umbugs ."

"An' shu'll 'ave nowt ter do wi' comers-in."

"Lots o' women die 'avin' their first bairn," the mother-of-eight shielded her eyes from the glare of the sun to stare at Sarah to see if her words were having effect. Satisfied they were, her sagging bosom and broad hips wobbled toward the High Street as she further elaborated on the horrors of giving birth to one's first child.

Autumn found Sarah big and round, like an overgrown fruit, suffering every night with backache from the strain of carrying little Amy, for she was sure it would be a girl. She would pause in the afternoon sun and watch the young children playing on the staithe, or the group of boys, ten or eleven year-olds, innocently naked and splashing among the breakers, darting between the waves like water-rats.

She was better in the fresh air than in the confines of the cottage, for here she could forget the silly stories that she'd heard. About the baby born with two heads, and the child with a pair of wings that had fluttered about the bedroom and when exhausted had fallen dead at the midwife's feet, its body limp and blue.

Then one November afternoon, with thunderous skies over a cruel pewter sea, she went into labour. Late that night, Cain having to ply old Lizzie with Geneva to persuade her that she really was needed, the old woman staggered up the stairs to attend to the "foreign woman".

Asserting her authority, she straightway ordered the father and grandfather out of the room to enable her to "see ter things". Garbed in black, she had a distinctly malevolent look, enhanced by the big blood-stained apron she wore for gutting fish and delivering babies. She took a good look, then banged on the floor with her stick.

"Shu'll be soom time yet," she delivered her considered opinion to the two men who had come racing up the flight of stairs. "Bin leadin' yer all on, I shouldn't wonder."

The mother-to-be felt another sharp pain, and drew her breath. She was not going to cry out in front of such an audience.

"Ah've tied this sheet ter 'top o' bed"—and Lizzie began to initiate a now terrified Cain Dacre into the secrets and mysteries of delivering babies. "Shu can pull on it when it starts comin', d'yer see."

Sarah's forehead was wet with sweat, her whole body racked with a terrible, all-consuming pain that she'd never before experienced. She could remember seeing animals in labour, she'd even helped a cow to calf, but now she was experiencing for herself just what bringing a new life into the world was all about. And, for some reason, Amy was not being at all cooperative…

Two hours later Lizzie, still in her fish-gutting apron descended the narrow stairs to announce that she was "goin' ter privvey". Looking at the Dacres, for the rest of the family were huddled round the fire, she explained, "Ah've gi'en 'er two penn'oth o' laudanum, an' Ah'll look in first thing. It's goin' ter be a bad time for 'er, Ah'm feared—an' Ah mun be away afore Ah pittle me breeches."

Then at the door she paused. "If owt 'appens, fetch me."

Cain suddenly jumped up. "But yer can't go 'ome, Lizzie, not wi' Sarah—"

"Allus trouble wi' first 'un." Lizzie spoke from long experience. "But shu's been tryin'. Shu needs soom rest. Remember Ah'm nobbut a few doors away."

The following morning, as the Dacres were about begin another day's chores, Lizzie re-appeared. "Well, an' what's ter do?"

"No change."

"Well, Ah've soom 'elp coomin. Dorcas thro Bells Bank. Yer'd best be away afore shu arrives." And the old woman, who had spent over half a century bringing infants into the world, shuffled upstairs to the business in hand.

A desperate cry made her hurry, and on entering the bedroom she drew back the bedcovers. Minutes later the head began to appear. There was another cry, the child's head again descended, and Sarah was torn with an all-consuming pain as Amy struggled to be born. Breathing became frantic, her body riven apart by a vortex of pain.

"Push, Doy," a voice encouraged her. Dorcas, Lizzie's helper, had arrived, watching in amazement as she always was on seeing the midwife deliver a tiny bloodstained thing. She who'd been at the birth of half the population of the village, drew forth the child, cut the cord, then laying the infant on the bed saw… a baby girl.

She was limp, neither was she breathing. With Dorcas trying to give advice, Lizzie lifted up and slapped the frail bundle.

There was nothing!

Then, after what seemed an eternity, a quickening—the first spark of life. Gnarled old fingers traced the gap in the infant skull where the brain throbbed visibly. The baby was alive and breathing. Young Amy was cleaned and wrapped in a warm blanket. Then, after the two women had attended to the mother, by now exhausted but blissfully happy, Lizzie announced, "It's a girl."

"Can I see her?"

Proudly the old woman cradled the child and placed her in her mother's arms. "Just thee 'old then, afore we do what we allus do wi' Steeas bairns."

"What's that?" Sarah asked in alarm.

"Dooant thee fret, Doy," Dorcas was quick to calm her. "We mun tak' 'er up in 'attic an' 'old 'er aloft. That's so as shu'll go up in 'world."

Later that day, when the menfolk returned from their day's fishing, mother and baby were lying in the four-poster. Sarah was beginning to realise just how foolish she'd been to take any notice of the silly tales she'd heard about Staithes babies being born with two heads and the like. Little Amy was fine: she was absolutely perfect.

After her lying-in, the child was christened.

The following winter was one of violent storms and the Dacres were not able to put out to sea. Boats were hauled up the slipway or tied up in the beck, and on empty bellies the household grew fractious. There was no money, nor was the mainstay of their diet to be had, for not even the Dacres dare take to the water. They, like the rest of the village would, at high tide, collect and fight over whatever driftwood the sea had thrown up, the head of the household miraculously finding money for ale every night.

Cain marvelled at that, and envied him. All he had was the constant screaming of an infant, and a wife who, not having given him the son he'd so hoped for, he now cared little about.

Then one night, when the wind was howling and blowing spume against the windows, he could stand it no longer. In a fit of blind, uncontrollable fury he flung the defenceless bundle across the bedroom and against the wall.

Suddenly the storm abated. Momentarily stunned by his own actions, he stared aghast at the tiny baby. He came nearer in order to witness the terrible act he'd committed. On the wall, like the innards of some fish he'd gutted, were the brains of his daughter. The head was split open and he brought his hands to his face to try to wipe out what he'd done.

Then there were footsteps behind him, and a scream that would haunt him forever. Sarah stood stock still, scream after scream coming from her throat.

"Shut up, bitch!" But although he hit her again and again, the sound grew worse as, like a thing demented, Sarah stood over the pitiful bundle that had been alive only minutes earlier.

Then, realising his action, and fearful of the consequences, Cain rushed past her and down the stairs as the rest of the Dacre household came in to see what he'd done. Strong arms reached out as Sarah slumped to the floor.

The next thing she knew, she was sat in a chair near the fire and being made to drink sweet tea. Then she heard her father-in-law saying, "P'raps 'bairn fell."

"No dad, tha knows better." Aaron, forever jealous of his elder brother, grasped the opportunity with both hands. "Bairn wor brayed ageean 'wall if tha wants my opinion. An' when Cain's up afore magistrates, they'll 'ang 'im. They'll try 'im at York Assizes, an' find 'im guilty as 'ell."

"We'll 'ave less o' that talk. We mun wait… till Cain comes 'ome."

"*If* 'ee comes 'ome."

"Sarah, what 'appened?" Aaron insisted.

"He just… picked her up… and threw her—"

"I told thee. Nah…" The younger brother was enjoying bringing down the firstborn. "Ter late fer 'doctor—is it ter be 'undertaker? Magistrates? What do we do?"

"We wait fer Cain."

But several hours later the bidder was to be heard in the village, standing outside the door of family, friends and relatives, calling, "Will yer coom? Will yer coom ter a little mite's funeral? For Cain and Sarah Dacre's bairn as bin called ter 'er maker." And several days later the whole of the village, so it seemed to the shocked mother, turned out for the funeral of baby Amy.

Isaac Dacre, who had taken it upon himself to make sure there would be a decent bringing forth, placed the tiny white coffin on a small table outside the house, as mourners, family and friends were arranged for the procession that must make its way through the village. His eyes darted here and there, but there was no sign of the father. His son was not merely a murderer, but a coward.

The bawler struck up and the villagers joined in the singing of a hymn. The coffin was lifted and, as was the custom, eight girls robed in white preceded the innocent little corpse. They carried garlands of coloured ribbons and in the centre of each was a white glove, marked in the palm with the age of little Amy. Three months.

Sarah, still in the world but no longer part of it, moved with the cortège as it made its way to the churchyard in nearby Hinderwell.

Even when the dreadful affair was no longer the focal point of Staithes scandal, there was still no news of Cain Dacre until, months after the event, there were vague reports that he'd joined a whaling ship. Then came another tale that he'd fallen foul of the impress-men and was now serving in one of His Majesty's ships.

Sarah, not knowing which way her life was to turn, took little interest in the rumours, and in a world of her own would stand on the edge of Penny Nab on the pretext that she was "looking for his ship". Wishing she had the courage to jump. To end it all.

Isaac Dacre had tried with her. More than once he had taken his belt to her in an effort to bring the lass to her senses, but to no avail. Until finally he washed his hands of the whole business. Provided she continued to look after the house, she'd have a roof over her head—leastways until he heard something definite about Cain.

Cain Dacre! Even the very thought of the man was distasteful to her. And as Sarah looked at a pile of socks that needed darning, she imagined what her life might have been like if it had been Tom Metcalfe she'd met at the Hiring Fair.

If only…!

Chapter 8

Tom went several times to the mill—and on occasions even ventured into Staithes in the hope of seeing her—but Sarah, it seemed, was to be no more than a figure of his imagination. Was she real? Had he met and made love to her that afternoon, or was the mind playing cruel tricks?

He thought of Leah and Ashley, who had only one topic of conversation, but all the same were unable to settle on a date for their wedding until their new home was ready. And then there was Constance, and Lynton Shaw, who might be years before they could wed, and…

And anyway, Sarah was already married, and there were lots of unmarried eligible young women in Whitby who'd jump at the chance, were he to court one. A shopkeeper's daughter perhaps? She would be such an asset when Leah and Ashley did finally name the day.

But he thought of the afternoon sun darting through the canopy of leafy trees, and how willing his partner had been. He wondered if all women were the same, but straightaway dismissed such a notion.

Sarah was special. What they had done that afternoon would remain with him for ever. To take another woman for his wife would seem to him as second best.

But he had to try hard to concentrate on the matter in hand, for with Stanhope as their advocate, he and Leah would, more than likely, have an apprentice before the month was out.

"Gentlemen of the Board, and guardians of this very worthwhile—and I must regrettably add, *necessary* institution"—and the thunderous voice paused for effect before lunging into the well-rehearsed oratory. For Stanhope Langden was, besides being a learned man of the law, a theatrical figure: a ringmaster full of his own importance.

"I crave your indulgence and valuable time, as I hereby set before your goodselves the nature of this petition on behalf of my client, to whom I shall convey with all possible speed your decision (or even recommendations!) as the Board may see fit to make.

"My client, Sirs, is a most highly respected figure in the town, pursuing the calling of an apothecary. He is an upright, law-abiding member of society; a member of the town's militia; and because of the most generous offer he is making today must indeed surely be a gentleman and a man of altruism. For he is prepared not only to feed, clothe and house some unfortunate orphan boy… but also to teach him a trade!"

He paused for effect, before continuing.

"The said boy shall need to be no less than ten and no more than twelve years of age, and be able to read and write. Furthermore my client promises, as yet a further gesture towards his integrity, that after a trial period to assess the boy's suitability to such a calling, he should be indentured to him, with relevant papers signed and witnessed by the Board.

"Furtherto and in addition, the boy is to reside at my client's home, and live with my client and his sister as part of the family, where he will, in short, enjoy the benefits of a stable home life and a Christian upbringing. He shall be schooled by my client and duly initiated into the arts of being an apothecary, being privy to the special knowledge that such a calling entails.

"I thank the members of the board for their valuable time, and feel I should not impose on them further, but humbly await their decision."

And in a manner befitting his calling, Stanhope Langden, having presented his case to the very best of his ability, and knowing the persuasiveness of words, but also the power of silence, withdrew while the board deliberated.

Some two weeks later Tom and Leah made the journey from Church Street to Green Lane and the town's workhouse. Built some ten years previously by subscription, it replaced the building that had stood on a piece of waste ground close to the harbour near the opening at Boulby Bank. Though it could arguably be said to be in a more pleasant and spacious position, it was still the town's workhouse.

Another such building, the Ruswarp Workhouse, was under construction in nearby Stakesby Road. Tom half-wondered if, there being no suitable lads at Green Lane, perhaps Stakesby Road would provide the new apprentice. He would need to be…

But then Tom thought of the brother and sister who'd unexpectedly presented themselves at Nathaniel Stottard's many years ago. Tom, having grown up on a farm, had never expected events to turn out the way they had. And now, he and Leah were able to make good the debt they owed for it, and repay their uncle's kindness, by offering a home to another unfortunate lad.

Leah must have read his thoughts, for she suddenly took his hand. "He'll be all right, you know, this new helper we're going to get."

"Let's hope he is."

"Yes, he will be, Tom. He'll be able to… sweep up and things, and run errands, and even amuse uncle Nathan when we're both of us busy, and he can also—"

"Poor lad's going to be rushed off his feet," Tom joked. "At this rate, we're going to need two."

"Oh no! One will be enough."

"But what if… it doesn't work out as we hope it will? If we take some orphan lad and give him a home for, say, a couple of months, then find he's not suitable. What happens then?"

"But that situation is not going to arise. We're going to choose some boy who's… oh, I don't know how to put it, but when we see him, we'll know he's the one. Come on Tom, be sanguine."

He looked at his sister, dressed in her finest so as to create a good impression, and thought again of the good sense of having a helper about the place. Especially as Leah would—possibly only a few months hence—be a married woman and living in the fine house in Bagdale.

He took a deep breath. His mind was made up.

Minutes later, in the cold comfort of the town's poorhouse, a number of boys were paraded for their inspection. They ranged from six- or seven-year-olds to others close on being young men, yet all of them subservient and bearing the mark of an institution such as they now had to yield to.

A clerk wearing a ridiculous wig, and picking a syphilitic nose, called out a name, and a lad stepped forward, while a member of the Board gave a brief history of the young man and also extolled his virtues. "A big strong lad, you'll have no—*hands by your sides, boy!* Now, where was I? Ah, yes: father was a sailor, mother… a 'professional lady', by all accounts." He gave a look that spoke volumes, then added, "This boy will give you no trouble. And he can read… and write."

"Walters," the clerk called out as he scratched under his headgear, and the next lad came forward.

Tom looked at Leah and followed her glance to a pathetic fair-haired boy standing toward the end of the line. He was thin and pale, probably nine or ten, and had a look about him of such sadness that Tom could tell why Leah had already made her choice.

Tom half-listened as the member of the board boasted that this "bright young man can do arithmetic and eats very little" or that another "reads his bible every day and would be a credit to any employer." Some others, upon being called, showed samples of "their" handwriting, or "read" poems they had earlier learned by heart.

"Duncan Sykes," the voice called, and the fair-haired lad swallowed hard, then shuffled forward out-of-line.

"How old is this young man?" Leah straightaway wanted to know.

"Ten years and two months, Miss," a puny voice replied.

"Quiet, boy!"

"…And you can read, and write?"—Tom ignored the clerk's command. Taking a slim volume from his pocket he opened a page, handed the book to the young lad and said simply, "Read it for me."

The index finger followed the lines on the page. There were only one or two words where the lad faltered. Tom looked at his sister, then said, "Thank you, Duncan. I'd like also to see a sample of your handwriting, if that's possible."

Leah nodded in approval. Their minds were made up.

The formalities completed, all that remained for Mr and Miss Metcalfe to do was to take the boy home with them.

"And may I compliment you on your good choice." The overseer of the poorhouse bowed respectfully as Tom and Leah stood in the hallway, waiting for Duncan to join them. Then they heard footsteps and the boy appeared. Leah smiled, "Are you ready?"

"Yes, Miss."

"Come on then, let's get you home, and we can have muffins for tea. Do you like muffins, Duncan?"

"Don't know. Never eaten any."

Leah put her arm round him. "With lots of butter, and damson jelly?"

"You'll get this young man fat,"

Then, as their new life began and the three of them left the poorhouse and walked down Green Lane and into Church Street, Duncan burst into tears. Leah put her arms around him.

"Come on then, what's the matter? Don't be afraid, Duncan, for you're safe with Tom and me."

"I'm sorry, Miss… sorry, Sir—but I'm so happy now."

"And that's another thing—you must always call me Tom. Not even Mr Metcalfe, and certainly not 'Sir'. And if we're all going to live as one big happy family, then this is Leah. You're going to be part of the household, so it's first-names from now on."

"And we must get you measured for a suit of clothes," Leah fussed, "and nice new aprons to wear in the shop."

"But first things first, young man. We need to get you in a bathtub of hot soapy water, and then deal with those 'lodgers' you've got in your hair, and—"

"And you need to meet uncle Nathan," Leah skilfully diverted what could have been more tears. But Tom was quite correct: even she was beginning to scratch the crown of her head.

The three of them made their way along Church Street—and Duncan stared in awe at what was to be his new home. Tom Metcalfe heaved a sigh of relief. Having the lad might even—*would*—help him forget *her*—the earth-goddess that had, only weeks before, captivated and seduced him. Sarah whatever-her-name had not only taken his virginity, she had also robbed him of his appetite, disturbed his sleep, invaded his everyday thoughts and his…

Oh—what love could do to a man!

Constance Langden also was a victim of Cupid's dart. She stared at her reflection in the pier glass mirror and imagined she was suddenly seeing Lynton.

He was coming toward her, she could feel his kisses on her shoulders, and she turned her head toward him as his hands caressed the front of her gown…

But there was no Lynton Shaw in the drawing room, only in her mind. And she sighed, as she began her weekly letter to him.

> *My darling Lynton,*
>
> *I count the hours, the days until we can be together, and all the while we are apart my love for you grows, and each night I pray to God that he will you and your ship and keep both from harm.*
>
> The Times *and the* Leeds Intelligencer *frequently carry reports on that scoundrel Napoleon, and it would seem that should he try to invade, then it would again (as in his previous and futile attempts) be either Wales or Ireland where his forces might land. Since the self-opinionated individual declared himself an Emperor and organised his coronation in Reims Cathedral his ego daily grows. I also read somewhere that his cape is now embellished by over three hundred gold bees that had once decorated the cloak of King Childerich and had been removed from Toumi Cathedral for that purpose. Vanity!*
>
> *I also hear of his latest boast that "the Channel is but a ditch, and anyone can cross it who has the courage" and he further goes on to say "let us be masters of the Straits for six hours, and we shall be masters of the world".*
>
> *What a truly insufferable man this self-styled dictator is, and how is he tempting fate by already having a medal struck in order to reward his victorious troops for conquering England—oh, that I were a man and able to*

> come in mortal combat with this monster. All I shall say is, if he or his troops should dare to land on our shores, then he had best beware.
>
> I also understand that to warn of any possible attack a chain of towers are to be built on what are deemed to be the most likely invasion beaches, each tower to mount a single gun that could offer cross-fire to the landing troops. The aforementioned towers are to be round and tapering, and thirty feet tall with the outer sea-facing wall over twelve feet thick. Built on three floors with the entrance to the first floor reached by a ladder that can be pulled inside and raised during a possible siege, the first floor is to be the living quarters for a garrison of twenty-four men, the ground floor being used to store food and ammunition.
>
> Do you think Whitby will be one of these towns?
>
> And now, for news nearer to home. Ashley and Leah are making plans for their forthcoming wedding. Their new home is to be furnished in a grand manner and they are employing local craftsmen as and where they can for the re-decorating. I try not be jealous, telling myself that when your five years of enlistment comes to an end, then we can become husband and wife.
>
> I do so love you, my darling Lynton.
>
> Your ever-loving Constance.

Lynton read the letter yet again, and placed it on the table in front of him so that he could refer to it as needs be, as he began to compose a reply.

> My dearest, dearest Constance,
>
> Oh, how I wish that you were in my arms, and hearing the words of love I long to whisper to you and you alone. God speed the day when we live as one, for truly my life belongs to you.
>
> I have what, for us, could be good news. The ship is to dock in London at the end of the month to undergo repair work, and as the overhaul will take several weeks to complete, we may well be able to meet. It could well be that I am unable to leave London, but perhaps you might join me, and together we could see the sights that London has to offer.
>
> Looking forward to your reply, and sending you all my love.
>
> Lynton.

He re-read his letter. It was brief and concise, nor did he see any sense in alarming her at this stage regarding the sudden deterioration in his wellbeing. A "sea voyage" might well be beneficial to a man in his condition, were it not for the sickness and disease that was all around him. Men with open sores that stubbornly refused to heal; others with the venereal pox, which among the crew and even the officers on the ship seemed rife—and there was another sickness among the men, and he seemed to have fallen an unwary victim to this malady.

His recent weight loss, breathlessness, slight fever in the evenings and night sweats, together with a persistent cough and blood-specked sputum further convinced him that he was suffering from what the Greeks called *phthisis*...*

He shuddered when he remembered that Hippocrates had strongly advised his students against treating it. It was incurable, progressive and terminal—and a corpse was bad for business.

---

* TB.

Chapter 9

The morning air was sharp and clean, the cobbles around the Town Hall glistened as Tom and Duncan walked from Sandgate toward the steps leading up to the abbey. Duncan wanted to count them, just as Tom had often done when he'd first arrived in Whitby.

Though he'd been with them for only a month, it seemed as though he'd always been part of the family, and had certainly been made to feel welcome by uncle Nathan. The two of them giggled as they shared secrets, and the lad's arms would affectionately embrace the old man, as his uncle playfully rustled the head of blond hair.

In smart white apron the lad looked every inch as though he was born to the job as an apothecary's assistant, and any earlier thoughts of the possibility of him being unsuitable and being sent back were now completely forgotten. Duncan was here to stay, and was now being instructed into the ancient art of this form of medicine.

"Apothecaries," Tom had explained at the very outset, "are considered to be doctors. Our main responsibility is to prepare medicines and the like, but we do also visit, and are consulted by, the sick"—and Tom had thought of his own early days, and being instructed by his uncle in the preparation of herbs, and heard again his uncle's affirmation that "'erbs mun be married one wi' another to bring about a cure".

An apothecary kept a journal of remedies called a *pharmacopœia*, listing ingredients, preparation and dosage. Tom did so, as his uncle before him had done. Most remedies were based on the *Doctrine of Signatures:* the conviction that the shape of plant would be beneficial to that ailing part of the patient that it resembled. Almonds were good for the eyes, walnuts for the brain and red rose-petals for the blood.

No formal schools existed to train apothecaries: learning was by apprenticeship to such a person only. Tom was prepared to teach Duncan all he knew eventually, things like bleeding and blistering, but as-and-when these were needed.

"Fourteen, fifteen, …" the lad counted out aloud. "Six—come on, Tom. Sixteen, seventeen, …"

"Keep going, and keep counting"—for Tom had stopped and, looking along Henrietta Street, fancied he recognised… but his mind was surely playing tricks.

Besides, why should she be in Whitby, so early in the morning?

"Thirty one, thirty two, …"

"I'm coming. See if you can count to fifty before I catch up with you." And Tom mounted the steps two at a time. "Forty four, forty six, …"

"And when we've reached the top and come all the way down again"—and Tom took deep breaths after his sudden exertion—"we'll go into Haggersgate and call at *The Star*. For there's a library in the rooms above, and we can choose some books for you."

The lad threw his arms around him—and Tom was suddenly the proudest man in Whitby. Being with Duncan was real. His preoccupation with Sarah amounted to chasing after what he couldn't have—and that did not make for a happy man.

Rushing to seek shelter in the shop doorway as she shook the flurries of the first winter snow from her outdoor clothes, Leah paused to look up at the December sky—and shuddered when she thought of Constance and Ashley who, several days hence, would embark on their journey to London to see Lynton Shaw. Constance, seeming very brave to Leah, had originally been planning to travel on her own, until her best friend suggested that Ashley accompany her.

"But that means you won't see Ashley over the Christmas period at all."

"Well, it'll only be for a few days… a week at most. And besides"—Leah sought for excuses to make things easier—"I shall have Tom and Duncan to keep me company. And uncle. When Lynton sails, it could be months and months before you see him again, and… London's a long way to travel alone."

Constance had to agree, and was pleased and relieved at the thought of having her brother accompany her.

As Leah took a look at the malevolent sky she did not envy the soon-to-be travellers. Not even the fine London stores Ashley had described, their windows displaying the latest gowns and mantles, could tempt her. Her Christmas would be spent in Whitby.

She hurried through the shop to their living quarters, where a delicious smell of cooking met her. For she'd had a busy morning—been busy for weeks, if the truth be known.

Christmas cakes, the Christmas pudding, gingerbread, making mincemeat for the pies—the more she could do now, the less there'd be to do as the day drew near. There would of course be the goose and the haunch of venison (unless she decided to cook a whole ham); a delicious trifle—and on Christmas Eve the traditional frumenty for the evening meal.

Earlier in the month, as was the local custom, young girls had strolled from door to door carrying their boxes of ornamental pasteboard on which was placed the wax doll, the image of Christ, surrounded by strips of boxwood and the obligatory two or three apples or oranges. Taking their stand at every door in the town (unless expressly forbidden to do so) the girls, with their vassell[*] cups would sing their carols, their upraised voices being a signal for the household's attention.

> *God bless your kith and kindred,*
> *May no ill you dismay.*
> *Remember Christ our saviour,*
> *Was born on Christmas Day.*
> *Glory to God, the angels sing,*
> *Peace and goodwill to men we bring.*

The singing would continue, ending with:

> *God bless your kith and kindred,*
> *That live both far and near.*
> *We wish you Merry Christmas*
> *And a happy New Year.*

Sometimes the singers were strangers, others familiar from previous years, and therefore doubly welcome, and after giving them some small gratuity, good luck for the following year was assured.

The following year!

Why—she'd be Mrs Ashley Langden, mistress of a fine house in Bagdale, and Constance might even have married Lynton. As for Tom?—well, perhaps by then her brother would have fallen in love with… oh, not the daughter of a parson or anything, or even a farmer's daughter, and she puzzled as she tried to imagine "the right girl" for Tom.

Of course, there'd also be uncle Nathan to consider—and there was also Duncan, and—and she must stop her fanciful thoughts and go out yet again to buy a loaf of bread. Three hungry men, there was no filling them. She'd also buy some muffins, Duncan liked them.

As she hurried along Church Street there was the clatter of horses' hooves and the sound of carriage wheels over the cobbles, and she stood watching the sudden burst of activity in the vicinity of the *White Horse and Griffin* as the travellers alighted.

---

[*] Dialect: c/f wassail.

There was a flash of white breeches from under a redingote as one of the gentlemen rushed forward to help a young woman step from the coach. Her velvet cloak trailed on the carriage steps as she carefully picked her way, only to be followed by an older woman swathed in furs and matching muff. There was such an air of breeding to the travellers.

Yet another member of the party, a gentleman with a bi-corne hat tucked under his arm and also wearing a flowing travelling coat began giving instructions to the waiting stable lads. They busied themselves, touching forelocks before picking up luggage, and removing from inside the coach travel rugs and copper hot water bottles.

Leah again thought of Ashley and Constance and their coming journey to London. She did not envy them. Not in the slightest.

The day drew nearer, the route planned with the precision of a military manoeuvre. They would travel on the daily diligence to Scarborough, and from there to Leeds, and at five the following morning from the *Old King's Arms* would board the *Balloon*, a new fast London coach carrying six passengers inside and one outside. Stopping at Leicester, where they would sleep overnight, they would finally arrive at *The Bull and Mouth* in London, early the following evening.

The fare from Leeds to London was, for inside passengers, two pounds twelve shillings and sixpence; for the outside passenger, one pound seven shillings.

Places on the London coach were already reserved. On their arrival in London, Lynton would be waiting for them, having reserved for them accommodation in the vicinity of his ship, should he be suddenly needed.

Constance kept her packing to an absolute minimum, telling herself that if the occasion demanded she could buy a gown on her arrival, and she would also, hopefully, be able to purchase ostrich plumes, ribbons and other accessories.

She must find a present for Leah, and also for Duncan—and she needed some gloves for herself. London, she'd been reliably informed, had the most amazing stores and emporiums—everybody should shop in London at least once in their lives!

The brother seemed more concerned than the sister on seeing his friend and soon-to-be brother-in-law, for Lynton Shaw had not only lost weight but also had an unhealthy pallor about him. Ashley noticed the persistent cough and more than once a sudden bout of breathlessness.

He spoke nothing of these things, but now that he realised something was amiss, he found himself constantly watching his friend, looking for other tell-tale signs. Lynton would make his excuses early in the evening and leave brother and sister to their own company. Ashley would pretend to be enjoying his glass of port, but his thoughts were on Lynton.

He pondered. Should he voice his concerns to Constance and risk spoiling their reunion? Better to wait until they were back in Whitby, where he could take Tom into his confidence and ask his advice before alarming Constance. Unless she too had noticed—and, like him, was keeping silent?

How long could the waiting game go on, before one of the players revealed their hand?

Like schoolboys they laughed and joked as they came into the shop, Tom ridiculously young for his years, and Duncan seeming very grown up in his smart new outfit.

"Now boys, just settle down, it isn't Christmas yet, not until… well, until we close this evening."

"Been busy?" Tom asked.

"Oh, two young ladies bought some of those coloured soaps we put in the window… and there's an 'elderly gentleman' keeps coming in and asking for you."

"Oh?"

"Giovanni. He's walking very painfully, to look at him. I think he's needing a jar of elderflower and goose-grease ointment, but daren't ask *me* for it."

A knowing smile came over Tom's face as he pictured the town's dancing master mincing along Sandgate. "Oh. Like that, is it? Poor Giovanni—he will be needing his long silver-headed cane to lean on."

"And I was thinking," and Leah seized the opportunity, "that Duncan might like to become a pupil of Signor Giovanni's. He holds dancing classes every week for the sons of gentlefolk and—"

"Daughters as well?" Tom asked the obvious.

"Of course, silly. Well, what do you think, Tom?"

"I think you're going to turn our young brother into a very smart young cockscomb. What do you think, Duncan?"

The lad looked scared. "Dunno. Will you come with me?"

"Oh, it's too late for me—but for a handsome young man such as yourself?—why, you'll have all the young women in Yorkshire madly in love with you when you grow up. You really should have all the social graces if you're to go mix with society and have girls falling at your feet."

"Saturday mornings"—and Leah considered the matter both settled and agreed, then added, "Oh, and I bought some bunches of violets from the woman who usually stands selling them at the bottom of Flowergate, by the Custom House. I thought you might want some to crystallise."

He nodded in approval and looked outside to see if any last-minute customers were lingering. In the fast-approaching dark, oil lamps and candles were being lit and placed in upstairs windows. "Another thirty minutes, say?"

"Then I'll go and lay the table for our evening meal."

"I'll start tidying and sweeping up".

"Good lad, Duncan—it'll soon be Christmas proper."

When the Town Hall clock struck the hour, Tom was about to lock the shop door and pull down the shutters when the woman who had all of a sudden become the topic of Whitby conversation came, somewhat unsteadily into the shop. She sashayed in front of the proprietor, swaying dangerously.

"Mrs Dalgleish, may I wish you the compliments of the season."

"Mr Metcalfe, as I live and breathe I must return your festive greeting, and should you *feel the urge* then we would be highly delighted if you would bestow upon my establishment the great honour of servicing one of my girls… or have both of them at the same time, free-of-charge you understand, as this is the Season of Goodwill." The coiffured and powdered head held erect, a hand clutched at the counter.

"Mrs Dalgleish, are you all right?"

"Oh, indeed!" Then she leaned closer and whispered confidentially, "Mr Metcalfe, do not judge us by our calling and profession, but rather by our frailties, for it is the mulberry wine that has been the ruin of many a good woman, myself included… and somewhere further along Church Street is Xavier… who will help me into my carriage… and I must wish you—oh, I already have done…! Silly me…"

Tom went to the door and looked out into the street. Instantly he caught sight of the young black man and called him over. He watched the two of them walk toward the *White Horse and Griffin*, where no doubt her transport awaited her. Then he locked the door: the Christmas festivities were about to begin.

Uncle Nathan was washed and dressed, seated in a comfortable chair near the fire and given a glass of mead. Lamps and the brightness of the fire lit the room, and when Duncan and Leah joined them, Tom ceremoniously placed the Yule log on the fire, while Duncan, under supervision, lit the tall moulded candle which was the traditional gift from chandlers to their clients.

Leah carried from the kitchen a large steaming bowl which was placed in the centre of the table, being the main dish of the evening. Frumenty: made of wheat, first steeped then boiled in milk, after which it was flavoured with spices and finally sprinkled with sugar.

Like an excited child, uncle Nathan clapped his hands when a bowlful was placed before him, then a good measure of rum was poured over it and stirred in. He even managed to feed himself, though he ate noisily.

Frumenty was new to Duncan, but he ate it nevertheless, and Tom persuaded him to have a second helping.

Then, when the dishes were cleared, the haunch of mutton and caper sauce and seasonal vegetables appeared, to be followed by lemonised apple pie and clotted cream, then cheese and gingerbread. Then, oblong in shape as a reminder of the cradle, their spices and fruits denoting the gifts of the Wise Men, came the mince pies!

Under the window, as in previous years, were the usual parcels wrapped in fancy paper to be opened the following morning, the only difference being that now there was an abundance of boxes and packages bearing the name *Duncan Sykes*, for Tom and Leah were determined that this would be for him a Christmas to remember.

At the end of the evening uncle Nathan was given a glass of port before being helped to bed, the Yuletide candle was snuffed out, and Tom did his usual rounds, going from room to room to make certain that fires were safe, and lamps and candles extinguished.

From her bedroom window Leah looked up at the stars and gave a wistful sigh. This would be her last Christmas as Leah Metcalfe, for soon she would be Mrs Leah Langden, mistress of the fine house in Bagdale. She counted on her fingers. Three—four months at the very most. She climbed into bed, blew out the candle and drew her bed-sheets around her.

Chapter 10

To Constance Langden the sights of London were truly breathtaking.

Fine buildings, the emporiums where one could, it seemed, buy just about anything and everything, providing one had the money, but more than any of these things, she marvelled at the spectacles London theatres had to offer.

The Covent Garden pantomime, *Harlequin Quicksilver,* with scenes including a Spanish seaport, a Spanish Square at Carnival time, a Masquerade in Madrid, a Fairy Palace and even a Silver Mine. Then the following evening at the Theatre Royal in Drury Lane, the pantomime *Cinderella,* directed by one Mr Byrne, with music by the celebrated Michael Kelly. Characters included ancient gods and goddesses, including Hymen, Cupid, Venus and various Graces. The Fairy Godmother's role was that of the Goddess of Love, one of the principal actors being Grimaldi, who played the servant role of Pedro.

The theatre was capable of containing an audience of almost four thousand people at any one performance. It seemed vast, with, besides an auditorium, a further five floors of circles and galleries, together with various boxes either side of the stage. She could well understand the well-known actress Mrs Siddons calling it "a wilderness of a place."

Oh—this would certainly be something to talk about for a long time to come!

And then there was the visit to *Astley's Ampitheatre* at Westminster Bridge Road in Lambeth, the circus arena being a breathtaking sixty-two feet in diameter.

Yet another highlight of the seasonal festivities was a new form of dancing called the waltz: something quite daring, as the couple held each other so very close and danced the opposite of "back to back". It took the basic foot pattern of a minuet, but differed inasmuch as the couples spun round the floor in mutual cooperation.

There was the dance tune *Duke of Kent's Waltz* and also *Nelson's Waltz,* besides dance tunes such as *Nelson's Hornpipe* and *A Trip to Canterbury,* and dancing in turn with her brother and her fiancé, Constance was quite exhausted by the end of the evening.

There was talk about plans for the following day—but more pressing for Constance was the talk she must have with her brother when the two of them were alone.

For she was worried… about Lynton.

Brother and sister, with Duncan running here-there-and-everywhere, as a young boy must, stared over a harbour swathed in scarves of fog coming from the Esk and wrapping themselves round ships' masts and riggings. Today was Childermas, the unhappiest, the unluckiest day of the year: a day when no boats would sail.

Though in the town itself there was still a feeling of Christmas and good cheer. There was laughter coming from the quayside taverns, even street vendors selling hot chestnuts, though the morning was cold and clammy, with a cruel wind and a sky that promised snow.

Leah hoped that Ashley and Constance would return in time for the New Year celebrations. For, truth to tell, she was beginning to miss him, and although she sympathised with Constance's situation…

Well, the following Christmas, Mr and Mrs Langden would be able to entertain all the members of both families from their house in Bagdale. And who was to say yea or nay to the supposition that Lynton would be among them? She imagined that, well, when he and Constance were married then, as Ashley had done, Lynton would relinquish his seafaring and the two of them would settle down to domestic bliss.

But to Lynton Shaw, who having said goodbye to his fiancée and her brother—and now, in an effort to raise his spirits, was in a quayside tavern drinking with his colleagues—marriage and all that it entailed seemed, like heaven, a world away.

With an air of bravado bordering on the euphoric, Lynton drained his glass, stared quizzically at the notice beside the ale-house door, then, trying not to sway as though he were on pounding seas carefully began to enunciate the message it contained. *"All true-blue British hearts-of-oak who are able, and no doubt able to serve their good King and Country…"*

"That's us, lads," Ship's Purser Jonathan Frazer broke in. He slapped Lynton and the third member of the slightly tipsy party Dick Scaithe on their backs, then clasped one in each arm. *"…All on board His Majesty's ships,"* Lynton continued, *"are heartily invited to repair to the* Roundabout Tavern, Wapping, *where they will find Lt James Ayesclough of* The Invincible *who keeps open house for the reception and entertainment of such gallant seamen who are proud to serve on board ships of—"*

"And look at that…!"—Jonathan again interrupted. *"All able seamen who newly enlist will receive three pounds bounty, ordinary seamen two, with conduct money, and their chest, bedding and the like sent carriage free."*

"*...Success to His Majesty's Navy, with health to the Jolly Tars of Old England.*" Dick Scaife read the final sentence, adding rhetorically, "God Save The King!"

"And God Save All of us... when the bloody cannons start."

The words came out without him realising, and the two men stared at Lynton as though he were confiding some deep naval secret. "I mean," he flustered, "well—you know, none of us are safe"—and he thought of the raw recruits seized nightly by the impress-men. Country yokels, some no more than young lads. Or pox-riddled layabouts that frequented the harbourside taverns. Seaport towns were dangerous places, if one valued one's freedom.

The moment passed, the three companions staggered into the night air, and feeling more tired than usual, Lynton made his excuses and headed for his lodgings. His careless remark had caused him to think—why? Why was he pursuing this career? And why with His Majesty's Navy?

The pay of a ship's surgeon was meagre. As assistant ships surgeon he had received three pounds a month. When surgeon proper it had risen to a princely five pounds, but on the debit side he'd had to provide his own instruments, which had cost nearly twenty five guineas.

Saws, and curved amputation knives, which made a circular sweep through the layers of flesh to the bone before the saw was used.

There was a screw tourniquet used to stem the bleeding prior to the actual severing of the limb, and haemorrhaging (hopefully) arrested by the use of the hooked *tenaculum*.

Also among his tools was a T-shaped *trephine*, this being needed to lift a compressed fractured skull, the T-shape being used to push the brain away from the wound. There were also *trocars* included in his implements for draining cysts and abscesses, tooth keys for extracting teeth, probes for locating musket shot and pistol balls or wooden splinters and other foreign bodies that needed to be removed. Apparatus for bleeding, and cupping for inflammatory conditions. And—because of a rule instituted by Earl St Vincent—a set of pocket instruments that a ship's surgeon must carry with him at all times, on-duty or off.

There were, besides surgical procedures, other things that became his "duties". Applying a rum-rub: the cure for a scorpion or centipede bite. Blood-letting. Treating pneumonia by the drawing of three pints of blood over a period of as many hours. Genito-urinary disease was rife—sexually transmitted diseases led to the development of urethral strictures, resulting in retention of urine, which needed to be released some other way.

Also in his surgeon's chest was a pewter *clyster*—a syringe for giving enemas, and which could also be used for flushing out the urethra for cases of venereal diseases, in the case of syphilis a mercuric solution being used to impregnate the urethra and bladder.

Strychnine was used as a stimulant. Drunkenness was rife—and he'd even heard tell of a rating who, having fallen overboard and apparently drowned and the body recovered, the surgeon had blown tobacco smoke into the man's lungs to revive him.

Working in a hospital, or even on his own account, must surely be preferable to his present employment. Even for a man of sound health it was an arduous occupation. Yet for one in his physical condition?—it was madness!

He re-read her letter, then putting pen to paper wrote:

My dearest, dearest Constance,

How precious our few days together, and how I so envy your brother being his own man. The sea can be a cruel master, but I must not dwell on such things, for soon, very soon now my five years service will be at an end. Other news much more relevant. The Admiralty are, in January, to introduce new measures to improve the lot of naval surgeons. Rates of pay and pension levels are to be increased, and uniforms similar to those of ships' physicians to be provided, and surgeons will no longer have to pay for drugs acquired from the apothecary.

His Majesty's Navy, so it would seem from posters strategically placed to attract most interest, is still anxious to attract new recruits, and one of the posters (which had been removed and I found in a gutter) I rescued and hereby send you copy of the details contained therein:

> *The old Saucy* SEVENTH *Light, or* Queen's Own Regiment *of* **Light Dragoon Guards**, *commanded by that gallant and well known hero* **Henry Lord Paget**.
> *Young fellows whose hearts are high to tread the* **Paths of Glory** *could not have a better opportunity than now offers.*
> *Come forward then, and* enrol yourselves *in a* **Regiment** *that stands unrivalled, and where the* kind treatment *the men ever experienced is well-known throughout the whole* **kingdom**. *Each* **Young Hero** *on being approved, will receive the largest* **bounty** *by Government.*
> *A few smart* Young Lads *will be taken at Sixteen Years of Age, five feet three inches, but they must be active and well limbed.*
> *Apply Sergeant Hooper.*
> N.B. *This Regiment is mounted on* **Blood Horses**, *and being lately returned from* SPAIN, *and the Horses* Young, *the men will not be allowed to* HUNT *during the next season more than once a week.*

I imagine the impress-men will be ever-vigilant in Whitby. Do tell Ashley to take great care, or he could end up in a position not dissimilar to my own.

I count the hours till we can be together again.

Your ever-loving Lynton.

Constance read, and re-read the letter, before methodically filling it away with all the other letters she had, over the years, received from Lynton.

She sighed wistfully. If only…!

Chapter 11

Constance was not the only recipient of correspondence, that day. As she stood on the shore watching a cormorant dive, Sarah Dacre, away from the prying eyes of her in-laws, took the envelope from her pocket and again read the contents.

Her father, only months previously having buried his second wife and once more "alone", was again making demands on her. But, she consoled herself, if she were to agree to his request she would be able to escape the austerity of this fishing community. This community that, on every possible occasion, made her feel she was an intruder—even her in-laws, especially since the disappearance of her husband after he'd killed their baby. It was as though they held *her* responsible for Cain's actions—and there was something else…

Cain's brother Aaron had, on several occasions, offered to "tak' 'mi brothers spot an' look after thee"—and would knock on her bedroom door late at night, hoping she'd allow him admittance.

The Dacres really were a law unto themselves!

She looked out onto mists swirling like vapours from a giant chalice, onto whispering waves and an impassive sky, and a sea murmuring, at times hauntingly, but now it was a monotonous song. The cormorant suddenly re-appeared and, rising from the water gave its long neck a sharp twist. There was something in its pensive loneliness that attracted her, as once more it submerged, while the tide, like a sheeted ghost, crept insidiously over the seaweed-covered scaurs of rock.

Sometimes on the stretch of shoreline she'd find a seal that had been washed up, only to be clubbed to death by the villagers, believing them to be at best predators and at worst witches in disguise and about their business.

But today there were no seals, just the cormorant.

Carried along in the wind was the rattle of the slow waggons from the ironstone mine further along the cliffs, where yellow foam spilled onto the scaurs, and on clear days spoil-heaps were visible, red and blue to ochre and bronze.

And above the sights and sobbing and subsiding of the sea Sarah fancied that she could hear and see something else: the sounds of the farm at Sleights—wherever that was. She could smell warm milk, feel the tongue of the newborn calf lick her hand, see the ungainly young goslings and cayed lambs, hand-reared and warm beside the kitchen range.

Too bad for her father, if he really was as ill as his letter was leading her to believe. But propitious for her—if it could be instrumental in bringing about her escape from the Dacres. Nor did she need to reconsider her instant decision, for there was nothing to commend her present situation.

That evening she bundled up her clothes and the few possessions she had, and the following morning at first light she crept from the house while the Dacres slept. It seemed to her, as she climbed the steep bank, that the entire village was asleep. Not once did she look behind her, nor had she left a note, nor any indication as to her actions. Her in-laws, she felt sure, would not trouble themselves as to her whereabouts, for they were now free of her, as she was of them.

Later that day, cold and weary, she stood in the kitchen of Far Clough Farm. Wilf Gibbons, now an old man swathed in blankets, stirred from his chair, stared, and before the apparition could vanish queried, "Sarah?"

"Aye, dad, it's me."

"But… 'ow did yer know… ?"

"This letter"—and she fumbled in her pocket. "From Jake… can't make out his last name. But you employ him, from what he says."

"Oh, aye…"

"You'm coomed up in the world"—and Sarah looked around her at the fine carved oak, swathed though it was in months of dust and neglect. He'd married well.

"Phoebe, God rest 'er soul, were what you'd call a woman o' property. Three farms in the area, an' various cottages as bring in a fair rent. But what good's that? When…"—and he paused to draw breath—"when you'm ill like me, money means nowt."

"At least," Sarah dismissed his self-pity, "you got the means to pay for doctors and—"

"Too late—me days is numbered."

"Then we'd best see to the fire and get a hot meal made, so's you can die in comfort." And she removed her shawl and set about bringing some semblance of order to what were to be be her new surroundings.

"I'll go and see to upstairs later—but what about the farm stock—feeding and the like?"

"Jake sees to all that. They'm all bedded down for the night."

"And first thing tomorrow I mun get a doctor to—"

"No!"—and he shook his head emphatically. "No doctors, please."

"But we mun see about this shortness o' breath. You gettin' chest pains?"

He nodded. "…An' coughin' an' chokin' all the time I'm in bed. So I sleeps sat up in a chair."

"That's no good. Tomorrow morning I'll call in at Whitby and get you—"

"An' 'ow's that 'usband treatin' thee?" he abruptly asked. "Did 'ee mind thee comin' to look after me?"

"It's a long story, me and Cain Dacre, and it'll keep. Oh dad…" and she gave a sigh. "So much has happened—to both of us."

He nodded. "Can tha forgive me, for what Ah did?"

For a long time she was silent. So this was what her father wanted: absolution!

Suddenly a flood of hurt welled up inside her. He was asking forgiveness for selling her to the Dacres, being instrumental in forcing her to marry against her wishes and condemning her to a life no better than slavery in the Dacre household. How could he even begin to atone for the wrong he had done her?

A mist came to her eyes as she held back her tears, and in a voice that sounded strange, even to herself, she managed, "nay, dad, but there's nowt to forgive."

"Then tha'll stay for a few days? 'Till Ah'm on me feet ageean?"

She nodded, and as the owner of Far Clough eased himself out of his armchair, Sarah began her tour of inspection.

Thanks to his second marriage, her father was indeed a man of substance!

Chapter 12

The ships looked a sorry sight as the waters of the Esk, brown and turgid, lapped against their sides. The January skies, heavy with snow, hung over the town like a tented canopy above a giant four-poster, the ships' masts being the supports for the same.

The strange stillness held an echo, as though it were a warning, but Duncan's feet marched in-time to the song he was humming. The lad's face glowed from the brisk walk, and Tom and Leah had to hurry to keep up with him.

Any subservience he might once have had about his person had completely vanished. He was now a 'Metcalfe'—Tom and Leah's young brother—and, as such, was treated like any other family member. Stanhope Langden, on being asked to draw up documents to legalise the change-of-name, had seemed more than surprised at what he termed "such a drastic measure". But he had complied with their request, and the forms had been signed and witnessed earlier that morning.

Duncan Sykes was no more: he had been reborn as Duncan Metcalfe.

He now had an assurance about him, coupled with a desire to learn, that was already proving an asset to the running of the business. He looked clean and tidy, was polite to the customers and, at the end of a busy afternoon, was fully prepared to help Tom sweep the floors and re-stock the shelves and drawers for the following morning.

In accordance with earlier statements made to the Board on Tom's behalf by Stanhope Langden, more papers were ready to be signed. Duncan Metcalfe—and from now on he was to be known only by that name—was to be indentured to him for the next seven years.

"Walk tall, gentlemens, head held high, shoulders back, as we approach ze young ladies"—and Signor Giovanni Torelli, one-time ballet master in France, now reduced to giving mere "dancing lessons" in an obscure part of Yorkshire, cast a critical eye over his "gentlemens" as they moved toward the empty chairs and imaginary dancing partners.

Suddenly he rapped the floor with his long silver-topped cane. "Stop right there. Look into ze mirrors. You are standing like… like cart 'orses, instead of gentlemens. We move… like *zis*"—and he struck an exaggerated pose, then walked toward the mirrors lining the far wall. "As we approach ze young lady, left hand held behind ze back—so. Ze right hand we offer, zis way. We give a slight bow, and smile. Big, big smile. We do it again, *si…?*"

As the "young gentlemens" tried to imitate him, Signor Giovanni nodded in approval. The tight silver wig was slightly askew, the cheeks rouged, eyes done up with kohl, and the knee-breechered, silk-stockinged dancing master automatically moved his feet into second ballet position as he surveyed his geese-soon-to-become-swans.

From the adjoining room, where young ladies were being coached by dancing-partner (and lover of many years' standing) Hortense, came the sound of a violin, the signal that the morning's tuition was to be be put into practice and the dancing proper could begin.

Duncan Metcalfe suddenly wanted to relieve himself, but thought better than to ask to be excused at that point. Dancing was all right for girls, he supposed, and it had been Leah's suggestion, not Tom's, that he present himself at Signor Giovanni's every Saturday morning. Besides, there was a big fat lad constantly trying to trip him up and make fun of him, and the "young ladies" were all giggly and silly.

Duncan was much happier behind a shop counter.

The apothecary's apprentice was eager, and in relation to anything and everything that he might spy growing in the hedgerow or some sheltered spot, he'd ask the same question, "What is it?" and then, "What's it used for?"

They had come upon a clump of gorse bushes that, for reasons unknown (not even to Tom) seemed to flower regardless of the time-of-year or season—and Tom, in reply to the usual question, would explain, "You can make wine from them, but it takes an awful lot of flower-heads and they're difficult to pick."

"And these?" and the lad would point to the furry green shoots that were appearing between the rough patches of couch-grass.

"Comfrey. Knit-bone, used for sprains and the like, and the root can even be boiled as a vegetable—though I've never eaten it."

And Duncan would stare wide-eyed at this fount of knowledge. "You know everything, don't you."

"Not quite," and Tom would laugh, then say, "But I do know it's time we made our way back, or Leah will wonder what's been keeping us."

He seemed to have completely changed their lives, for Leah loved him just as much as Tom did.

They returned to their shop just as the first flurries of snow started to fall. Duncan was hoping for a white Whitby, but Tom was more realistic, for snow rarely lingered on the coast.

The morning's customers came and went. Uncle Nathan, after a late breakfast, sat huddled in front of the fire. Until he decided it was time to inspect the harbour for enemy ships—but was persuaded to do it from the safety of his bedroom window, and only on the solemn promise that Tom would be the sole person to report his findings to the Admiralty.

Leah went out to buy some fish for lunch, Duncan having developed a liking for his fish fried. Today they would all of them have fried fish.

Tom looked in his leech jar. The residents looked remarkably fat and healthy—as they well should, having been fed the previous evening. Duncan had been horrified when Tom had explained how one "fed" a leech. But he was becoming quite used to them, and even seemed interested in their wellbeing.

"How much blood do they suck?"—had been his first question. His second, "Does it hurt?"

Tom had shaken his head. "No. Try one."

Duncan pulled a face. "I'll stroke it... but... "

"It'll bite you," Tom teased. "It'll bite your finger off."

"Take no notice, Duncan," said Leah.

"He knows it's only a bit of fun"—and Tom put his arm around the lad. "I wouldn't let *anything* hurt my brother."

"It's all right, Leah, I know he's just being silly with me."

The two young men struggled and pretended to fight. Tom realised just how much he loved the lad.

"And when the winter weather's gone, we'll take a boat up the Esk, how about that?"

Duncan nodded in approval. Then, just as they were about to begin their meal, the doorbell clanged as another customer came into the shop.

"I'll go," Duncan offered, but soon returned. "There's a lady wants to buy something for her father who's..." He blushed. "Well, anyway... I think she wants to talk to you," and Tom rushed from their living quarters, totally unprepared for what was about to ensue.

For the customer was Sarah, the young woman from Staithes!

For a long time they stared at each other. Tom hardly able to believe that it really was the woman he'd made love to months previously. Several times he'd imagined he'd seen her, only to be disappointed... but this time it was for real. He noticed her face change after the initial shock of their unexpected meeting, her earlier preoccupied frown was turning into a smile. He felt suddenly awkward.

Trapped!

"It's... Tom... isn't it?"

He nodded, just as Duncan came to join them. "And this very handsome young man"—and Tom tried to lighten the tension between them—"is my brother, Duncan."

"Hallo, Duncan."

"And Duncan tells me you're here to buy something for your father, who's—?"

"…Who has a terrible cough. Recovering from pneumonia—leastways, that what he says it was. I've only just found out that he's been ill, and he refuses to see a doctor, so I thought if I could get him something to help with his breathing—clear his lungs—it might… " She paused for breath, then asked, "What d'you think?"

"I could make up a mixture that will relieve his congestion. But if I were to come to Steeas and—"

She shook her head. "That's no good. Dad lives in Sleights. I'm staying with him till he gets better."

"Well"—and Tom thought quickly. He was not going to let her walk through the shop door and out of his life again, "If… me and Duncan happen to be in Sleights over the next few days, could I call and see how your father is? Difficult treating a patient if I don't know of his condition first-hand… It'd only take a few minutes but could make all the difference in the world to speeding his recovery."

Sarah considered it, then said, "Far Clough Farm. From here you take the path to Cock Mill then cross the Esk and head toward Sleights. The farm's along a track, but it's signposted. Do you know where I mean? There's some woods near Cock Mill, and—"

Tom nodded. "The woods are where the men from Whitby hide when the impress-men are active. It's well-known for it—but not to the press-gangs, mind."

"Then I'll tell dad… that you might call on him?"

"Tomorrow—unless we get a bad snowfall. What about you, Duncan? Fancy a day out?"

Duncan nodded. He'd go anywhere, so long as he could be with Tom.

"Now"—and Tom tried to appear professional. "You must scald these herbs that I'm going to make up for you, and I've a balsam he needs to inhale."

She sought in her bag then took out her purse—and Tom noticed the third finger on her left hand.

She no longer wore a wedding ring!

The following afternoon the Whitby apothecary and his young assistant presented themselves at Far Clough Farm. There they were offered refreshment before being led upstairs to see the patient.

"Dad's been ill for weeks—before I knew there was anything wrong with him. You see, I was in Steeas… and dad had re-married, and… now he's a widower again and no-one to care for him, so…" (she made a helpless gesture with her hands) "…here I am."

Tom wanted to ask… but thought better of it. Sarah would tell her tale, he felt sure, when the time was right.

"Have you any baby animals?" Duncan's question covered the sudden lull in the conversation.

"Soon—there'll be some lambs."

"And… are you managing the farm on your own?"

Sarah shook her head. "Dad has a couple of farm hands for all the back-breaking jobs, and… well, we get through between us. I grew up on a farm anyway, so it's not at all new to me."

"Sorry—" Tom stumbled, "I imagined… that you were from a fishing family."

She shook her head. "No." But she didn't elaborate.

As another cloud had come between them, Sarah suggested that Tom see her father. "He had some lawyer gentleman here a couple of days ago to draw up his will. Dad's leaving nothing to chance."

"That sounds ominous."

"Oh, I know dad. When spring comes he'll be right as ninepence!"

Tom saw that Wilf Gibbons had his doubts, but he kept his impression to himself.

"Duncan says he isn't hungry."

Tom stared at his sister. "Oh?"

"And he's sat in the back of the shop, all on his own, not looking very happy with himself"—and Leah pulled a face. She said, "but he might talk to you."

"Why, what's the matter with him?" Suddenly concerned, Tom jumped up from the dinner table and descended the stairs two-at-a-time to be with the lad, who had a sorrowful look about him and was huddled in a corner, taking notice of nothing and no one.

"What's up?"

The boy shook his head and looked away.

"Hey, come on. We're mates. What's happened?" And as Tom put his arm round him, Duncan suddenly burst into tears.

"You won't," and he sobbed, then tried again. "You won't send me away, will you Tom?"

"'Course not. Now, what's up? You did go to Signor Giovanni's this morning, didn't you?... and you were fine at breakfast... so...?"

"I've done something terrible..."

"—Knocked Giovanni's wig off?" Tom tried to make light of the situation, but Duncan seemed inconsolable.

"I know—you're sweet on some girl you've been dancing with... and she's fallen for somebody else. Oh, my poor little brother. A victim of Cupid's dart at such a tender age. But it happens to all of us."

Duncan shook his head.

"Well then, what have you done?"

"I've been in a fight."

"Who won?"

"I did."

"Well, then... d'you want to tell me all about it?"

"He kept calling me names... and..."

"Who did?"

"Timothy Langden."

"At Giovanni's?"

Duncan nodded, and in reply to the next question came out with the words, "He called me a workhouse brat, and said I'd no business mixing with people much better than I was, and so I—"

"Hit him?" Tom finished his sentence.

"I punched him in the face, and there was blood spurting from his nose and getting all over his clothes, and—you don't think he'll die, do you, Tom? I'm truly sorry and if you and Leah can forgive me I'll never hit anybody ever again."

"This is just for your ears, what I'm going to say now... I'm not at all cross. I'm very, *very* proud of you. But we mustn't let Leah know what I've told you. Is that understood?"

The lad nodded, and from his pocket took out a silk handkerchief to wipe his tear-stained face.

"And you don't have to go back to Signor Giovanni's unless you want to. But if you stay away, it'll look as though he's won, and if Timothy Langden makes any more hurtful remarks, even if he should see you in the town and start saying... then you have my permission to teach him a lesson, the fat little turd. It's time Westwood sent him to boarding school—and a long way away from Whitby. Now, come and get some lunch and take off those posh clothes. It's work this afternoon."

"What shall we tell Leah?"

"As little as possible. Let's keep this morning a secret. It's nothing to do with women—it's a man-to-man thing." And as Duncan threw his arms around him, Tom realised just how much he had become part of the family. He ruffled the head of blond hair.

"Duncan Metcalfe, we do love you"—and never had Tom felt more protective toward anyone than he did at that moment.

Smoothing things over with the Langdens would come later.

The dying flames in the kitchen gate at Far Clough made sleepy, flickering shadows dance on the rafters, as Wilf Gibbons heard her voice calling him again. Suddenly alert, he coughed and spluttered as he threw the covers from his makeshift bed and began searching for his clothes.

Still only half-dressed, he moved to where the glow from the fire reflected off the whiteness of the two orphans, who were snuggled together in their warm basket. As he knelt down beside them, a little black muzzle pushed itself toward the hand that touched it so lovingly.

All his many years of caring for animals and the land came into his mind: spring sowings, then golden harvests with waggons piled high, corn dollies and harvest suppers, and bitterly cold nights just as this one, when he'd been in the fields helping the ewes drop their first winter lambs.

The mothers huddled together, almost weighed down with the hard-packed snow clinging to their fleeces. Sometimes they'd even had to be dug out from under snowdrifts when winters were particularly fierce. He could well remember such nights and, straightening his back, he slowly moved towards the window to stare out into the blackness.

The stars shone hard and cold, and he momentarily paused as though undecided. Then, quite certain what he must do, he began searching for his outdoor clothes. His heavy boots were by the side of the hearth, there was a scarf hung behind the kitchen door next to his thick coat. He must hurry, for there was no time to lose.

A loving look at the lambs urged him on, for there could be some more out in the fields. He mumbled some half-articulate words to his charges, as might a mother to her child, then he donned his outdoor garb and unlatched the kitchen door.

The cruel night air momentarily took his breath away—it would be bitterly cold out on the moors. The stars looked down pitilessly as he crossed the yard and opened the farm gate. The stone walls glistened and the short frosted grass crunched beneath his feet as he crossed the field.

His breathing became irregular as something began to grip his throat. He stopped—but there was no turning back, for he was a man on a mission.

Again he fancied he could hear his wife Phoebe calling him. Perhaps she was already out there on the moors, and because of the insistence, and regardless of his own safety, he set out in entirely the opposite direction to where his two farm-hands, in the comparative shelter of the close, were attending to the lambing.

The owner of Far Clough wandered further and further. Over the winding moorland road, then, where the clumps of couch grass were like spun glass, the dead heather as candied frost, the ground, hard as iron began to rise. As though mocking him, the stars glittered and sparkled. And suddenly, full of malevolence, the night sky beckoned.

With hands of ice, and no longer any sensation in his feet, he struggled on, while all around him was an enveloping whiteness—and apart from that, nothing.

No sheep, no familiar landmarks, just haulms of hemlock with hoods of snow, the moorland rocks wearing diamond-crowned helmets—and the bleak, cruel vastness of the unsheltered moors.

Perhaps they'd strayed, or were on higher ground…

As he stepped forward, the first flurries of snow began to cover his clothing. Flake upon flake, spreading over him like a shroud. At the next group of standing stones he paused, looking out over the white world.

The snow persisted in clinging to the stubble on his chin, and again he heard Phoebe call out to him. He must find her, for it would be a busy night for the pair of them. Above the whine of the moorland wind he could hear her—her voice was clear…

"'Owd on lass, Ah'm a-comin'. Ah'll be wi' thee directly…"

The following morning, frozen to the earth, his body was discovered by Jake and Elias.

They carried him back to Far Clough Farm, where Sarah, drained of emotion, stared at the lifeless body. It was only what she and Tom had been expecting.

But, she began to realise, it left her in a somewhat uncertain position. Would she be able to remain at Far Clough, or be forced to throw herself on the mercy of the Dacres? And if Cain had returned to Staithes, would he come looking for her when he learned of her whereabouts? And… Tom Metcalfe had suddenly come into her life again—not that there'd been…

But what was she to do? What would become of her?

Three days later Wilf Gibbons was buried. It was a quiet affair, and in simple mourning garb she watched the coffin being lowered as the vicar mumbled prayers, then scattered earth over the coffin lid.

And life had to go on.

Later that day the animals at Far Clough were fed, the cows milked, eggs collected, and another orphan lamb brought in to join the other two. Only days later, Sarah was to learn her fate.

She was the sole beneficiary of the Last Will & Testament of Wilfred Gibbons, and now owned the farms, properties and various parcels of land he had inherited through his marriage. She had become a woman of substance.

Chapter 13

On that side of the ravine, seeming permanently in shadows from the overhanging cliffs, and the dwellings prised and squeezed between them, the incessant February rain came down. It seeped and oozed from the thatched and patched roofs of Staithes fishermen's cottages as though they were sodden sponges.

Rivulets sprang up among the steep ruttle track, merging into one ochre-stained artery as it channelled its sinuous way through the centre of the pathway leading down to the village proper. The water splashed and gurgled, then spewed over doorsteps and formed busy little pools before being carried with the main flow toward the cottages that faced seaward, before finally disgorging over the flat scaurs of rock as it reached the sea.

Roxby Beck, in full spate, and helped no doubt by the recent torrential storms, ran at a rollicking pace, carrying with it branches of uprooted trees, even the carcass of a stag, now swollen and stinking after several days in its watery grave, its antlers beckoning and trapping all manner of objects.

From above Boulby Cliff water gushed through the rocks. At one point it spurted like a whale, to be blown upward in veils of fine mist from the North Sea, making it appear as a trail of ascending smoke rather than a gushing, cascade of water. Shining and gleaming like polished granite, the rock face glistened with the soft spray, weeping in rivulets at its base.

The afternoon sky was low and menacing and Isaac Dacre, on leaving the alehouse, drew his breath sharply. The comfort of the bar and the generosity of the Preventative Officer (who, it was always arranged, would be miles further along the coast when contraband was being brought into the village, provided he had a share in the spoils) was infinitely preferable to his own home and argumentative sons. But there was *something* niggling him... and he paused from cursing the elements to blow his nose between his finger and thumb, wiping away the trail of mucus with the back of his hand.

"Bloody weather," he kept chuntering to himself as he lurched forward. "Blood weather... bloody... bloody weather."

For no reason, other than it was customary—*automatic*—for a Staithes fisherman, he meandered toward the slipway and cast a knowledgeable glance over the moored boats, then to the white water. Waves were breaking as far as the eye could see, and it would soon be high tide.

"God help anyone fool enough to be out on *that*," he muttered, for he knew full well that, young or old, experienced in seamanship or otherwise, a sea such as he was looking at made no distinction between men.

To Old Neptune, one was pretty much like another. Even if not taken by the extreme cold, then the business of trying to keep afloat whilst weighed down by heavy, cumbersome clothing would prove too much for anyone. Then, when the sea finally gave up its victim, more often than not the only means of identification would be the man's initials sewn into some item of clothing, so bloated and distorted would his features have become.

As Isaac slowly made his way to the village square, he suddenly supposed... if the body had not any item of initialled clothing, what then? How would a man's family know what had happened to him?—or that his body had been recovered? Or if... ? Supposing... a man changed his name, and joined some ship... and was at sea for many months, then when he came back took on another identity, then would he be the same man... or a man "reborn"? Would he still be hounded by magistrates and courts and the like for some terrible act he'd once committed in a fit of temper, or could he shake off his old life and misdeeds and begin anew?

But with a mark such as Cain had, how could that be disguised—unless the hand was chopped off?

A rope round the arm to act as a tourniquet, then a decisive swipe with a meat cleaver, and Cain Dacre would be no more. He could be... anybody. Anybody he wanted to be. He could pass his amputation off as a result of a whaling accident, or the price he paid whilst fighting for King and Country. Better having only one hand than the gallows.

But if a son were at best described as "missing", how could a father find out if he were alive or dead?

Safer perhaps to let sleeping dogs lie than start probing, and possibly stirring up trouble. Yet—and of this Isaac Dacre was certain—*someone* had been messing about with the boat. And if it were not Aaron or the two younger lads, then who could it be? And who would come into the house in the middle of the night and steal two loaves of bread? Rats?

But a rat wouldn't help itself to a bottle of brandy—unless it were a two-legged one. No, there was no doubt in his mind. Cain Dacre was in Staithes!

Or if not in the village itself, then certainly in the vicinity, and Isaac began to roam the alleyways and ghauts, looking for... he knew not what—but *something*...

"Now then," one of the villagers walked past, giving him the usual Staithes greeting. It could mean anything—or nothing—as befitted the occasion, and Isaac mumbled the same by way of reply. No asking the man if he'd seen the eldest of the Dacre sons, for that would arouse speculation and set rumours flying: the old fishwives in the village were always able to make something from nothing. His boots squelched and rain ran in rivulets down his back, but he seemed oblivious of these things.

Cain was somewhere—but *where?*

He searched high and low until, temporarily defeated, he reached the door to his cottage. He paused again to cast an expert eye over the crashing, pummelling waves and the surging foam, as spears of rain hurled themselves on the village. He'd get one of his lads to put up the shutters on the windows that faced seaward.

The wind was whipping up the waves. They were already splashing and spewing at the point where, at low tide, the flat scaurs of rocks were clearly visible. More than one ship had foundered over Penny Steel, her belly split in two, her cargo a prize for anyone daring enough to put out in a boat.

Isaac looked around him. So dark and malevolent were the skies, one could imagine it to be coming night, instead of the middle of the afternoon. He unlatched the door, and automatically called out, "Cain?"

He stood, listening to the silence—but he knew his lad was not far away.

Later that day the storm unleashed its full force upon the village.

The wind screamed round the rooftops. Roxby Beck, in full spate and carrying all in its path, spewed and crashed as it met the breakers being pounded against the cliffs and mouth of the harbour—and the wooden bridge spanning the beck was soon reduced to nothing but driftwood. Its sections bobbed up and down among smashed and splintered boats, and as each new wave flung itself against the seaward-facing cottages, great walls of grey spume thrashed and surged.

From upstairs windows could be witnessed skies riven by long forks of lightning, which further heightened the dramatic effect as they flickered over the sea and dived into the waves.

The Dacre family, seated around their fire, stared at each other in silence as above the raging elements another sound, low and menacing, was heard.

Suddenly there was a tremor as though the earth was moving beneath their feet. The door was blasted open as the maelstrom gathered momentum, and they heard a crash as one of the cottages was dragged into the sea. Isaac Dacre stared at his sons in horror and disbelief—yet there was worse to come. For the next flash of lightning lit up the village, illuminating a soaking wet individual outside their door.

"Look what the sea's spewed up!" Isaac Dacre spat out the words in greeting... as in walked Cain.

At first light the square was filled with a stupefied throng staring in disbelief at the devastation before them. The cottages, their foundations on no more than a sandbank, had stood little chance, and gaping holes in the still-standing, some now roofless, cottages made a pitiable sight. Perched precariously on an exposed roof truss, a toilet mirror, miraculously still intact, winked in the morning sunlight.

From the adjoining property, splintered floorboards protruded from a broken window. At their feet were items of furniture, two mongrels prancing among the rubbish, and an old man frantically searching for his flowered chamber-pot. A body had been recovered—that of old Annie Suckling. Someone suggested she had died of shock and that seemed to satisfy the onlookers.

Makeshift lifting gear was already being improvised. Four shire horses under the direction of the blacksmith were straining at the chains attached to the massive oak beams that were hampering the salvaging operation. Some men were steadying roof supports as they were dragged clear. All the while, as though mocking their efforts, the jackdaws paraded and preened themselves.

Across the village square there gurgled a trail of ochre water. Perhaps that had helped dislodge the foundations, someone suggested, for the water had been a nuisance for weeks. It could have been the main cause of the disaster, for it had rotted the wooden supports that had been driven deep into the sandbanks.

The horses, under their exertion, steamed in the early morning light, young men cursed, and onlookers freely voiced uncalled-for advice. Old women, garbed in their usual black, held up their hands prophetically as they offered probable and improbable causes for this visitation, and racked their befuddled old brains as they tried to recall even more dreadful and gruesome catastrophes, each hag trying to outdo her cronies.

One such foreteller of doom held out her dirty crooked finger to the others to gain their attention. Then the near-toothless mouth began to relate and embroider a tale her mother had told her, of an entire village swallowed up by the sea. Houses, the villagers themselves, their cats and dogs—nothing and no-one had been spared. And, she added for verisimilitude and good measure, her own mother had heard the bells—the bells which every year on that fateful day still peal out from Neptune's garden, putting those who hear them under their spell.

To hear the bells… one were as good as dead!

But Isaac Dacre had little time for such nonsense. He was here to listen to any gossip or rumours—that Cain had been seen in the vicinity. He was wiser than to broach the matter himself. Better to remain silent and pick up any clues to his son's escapades: for he'd not have returned to Staithes unless he were in trouble. He must keep Cain well-and-truly out of sight, until he could get rid of him… or the birthmark!

He hurried past old Margaret Ann and her companions. Garbed in black shawls and billowing aprons and looking like giant crows they cackled among themselves, old hags that they were.

The morning wore on. Isaac repaired to his boathouse—with a bottle of brandy for company.

Father and eldest son sat opposite one another, the dying embers in the hearth giving out a diffuse pinkish glow. Through the grey ash, the oil lamp illuminating the room cast long shadows as Cain suddenly roused himself.

"Another drink, dad?"

Isaac shook his head.

"Well, I'm 'avin' one"—and the contents of the bottle splashed the table before reaching the mug.

"That's it, lad, get blethered"—and the old man looked away. For he needed to keep a clear head. The drink—which would hopefully blot out what was about to take place—would come later, the following morning, when the act had been done. But for now he must remain sober and keep his wits about him.

He stared at his son. He had the Dacre features, but the nose, he supposed, might be a throwback to the Huguenot stock from several generations back. Their ship, sailing too close to the shore, had been torn to pieces as it drifted over Pot o' Steel some half a mile from the village, and the survivors had come ashore and eventually became part of the village and married and had families.

His own cousin, Louise, spoke little English—but fluent French. She seemed to spend all her time making lace, which she sold at very high prices to seamstresses who came from as far away as York, Scarborough, even higher up the coast—for her wares were in great demand. Cousin Louise was unmarried, still beautiful (in what he supposed was a 'French' way) and, he'd often thought—if he were to take another wife—she might have a tidy sum of money to bring with her. It was worth thinking about, when the lads were off his hands and… but that was in the future. Cain, at this moment in time, was the thing uppermost in his mind.

"Come on lad, let's fill thee up," and Isaac, disregarding the near-empty bottle, opened another. The figure sprawled over the kitchen table muttered something incoherent. Isaac grabbed his son by his hair and pulled the drooping head upright. "Come on lad—drink."

Cain tried to rise to his feet, but his father pushed him into the high-backed chair, and with a firm hand, began to pour the contents of the bottle down his son's throat. He began coughing and spluttering, but Isaac was not to be put off. The sooner Cain was dead to the world, then…

And he would thank him for it—yes, he would thank him… when it was all over.

Suddenly his head slumped forward onto his chest. Cain, now in a drunken stupor, was at his father's mercy. Isaac reached for the meat cleaver he'd earlier hidden, took a deep breath, then dragged the offending limb—the hand that set him apart from all other men, the only thing that could beyond doubt prove his identity—across the edge of the table. One swipe—there'd be a yell of pain with blood spurting all over—but when it was done, Cain Dacre would be Cain Dacre no more. He could be anyone he wanted. Nor would he be hounded down and sent to the gallows for killing his daughter—he would be a free man!

Isaac touched the edge of the cleaver. Oh—it was sharp!

Just one swipe—

But as he was about to do the deed, his victim suddenly stirred and, realising that something was about to happen, instinctively pulled his hand away as the blade sliced the table in two.

The following morning, whilst it was still dark, Cain Dacre again left Staithes, for Whitby. And there he joined the first ship to leave port—a whaler.

Isaac heaved a sigh of relief. He'd be away for many months… with a bit of luck, for good.

Chapter 14

From her bedroom window Sarah Dacre stared over the rolling acres of Far Clough Farm, which stretched further than the eye could see. So much land: she was indeed a woman of substance now. And there were other farms and rented properties, all part of her inheritance, and she had renewed her friendship with Tom— nay, more than that, for they were now lovers.

She should be the happiest woman in the entire world, were it not for one niggling thought. And this thought would come to her when she was lying alone in her bed at Far Clough, causing her to be on her guard, listening for the slightest sound. She would sometimes be awake all night or, during the day, she would look across the farmyard with its chickens guarded by the rooster—a Rhode Island Red—and half-expect to see him.

For he was no fool. And she was sure that word of her good fortune would have reached her in-laws, at least. But as for her estranged husband—if he were still her husband…? He could be dead, or have made a new life for himself somewhere—anywhere. How would she know?

But (and the thought terrified her) if Cain Dacre, still evading the power of the law, were in the vicinity—and word had reached him that his wife (and she still knew herself to be a married woman) was now a wealthy heiress—then might he not claim, or try to be part of, this wealth?

She had tried, though not very successfully, to discuss this with Tom, for he seemed to be more interested in what he could collect among the hedgerows. Or Duncan would be with him, which meant that he would not be able to stay the night. And she would retire alone to her bed and spend the night-time listening…

Tom Metcalfe was a busy man, for over the winter months the entire population of Whitby who had been gorging and swilling themselves sick, were now costive—and needing what some politely referred to as 'opening medicine', others being more explicit. There was also (and she seemed now to be a regular customer) Mrs Dalgleish, who would call on various pretexts, her latest being to purchase leeches. In reply to Tom's puzzled look she went on to explain confidentially, "To restore virginity. Four will be sufficient. A man of the cloth will be visiting my establishment later this week, and will hope to deflower my latest arrival, Rosalie.

She's very pretty and demure, Mr Metcalfe, and should you at any time…"

"Leeches? Mrs Dalgleish, how can leeches—?"

"They are cut, and 'strategically' placed—we need not say where—and when the gentleman's passions have been spent and his member withdrawn, there will be sufficient blood on the bed-sheets to convince him that deflowering has indeed taken place. Mr Metcalfe: the things one has to do! You wouldn't—you just wouldn't—believe it!"

"I take your word for it."

"And our professions are not entirely dissimilar—for you must have many young men coming to you with problems over their 'maypole'— the size, the rising, even recourse to surgery in some instances… And talking of surgeons, you must surely be familiar with Mr Langden. Such a gentleman of quality and refinement! But I have known the greatest—the very greatest—of London surgeons. When I worked in Covent Garden I was regularly visited and examined by these men… Oh—the tales I could tell!"

"Now, leeches"—and as Duncan returned from an earlier errand, Tom was anxious to be rid of his customer—"I'm awfully sorry, but I'm not able to help you on this occasion."

"Oh dear."

"Perhaps some other… er… *method* could be employed?"

She considered. "Yes, I think it could be arranged. It is a *difficulty*—but life is full of trials and tribulations, wouldn't you say? And worse things do happen at sea, they tell me."

She left the shop, Tom heaving a sigh of relief.

The new owner of Far Clough Farm felt, too, that life was full of trials and tribulations. Sarah Dacre once again tried to wrestle with her new situation and make some sense out of it. On the positive side she was a woman of means. And like many in her position could, if she so wished, boast of having a lover. She need never have any financial worries, and in Tom she had found everything she could possibly desire. He was handsome and attentive to her every need, especially when the two of them were side-by-side in her comfortable bed. A most ardent and considerate lover. Totally unlike—and she cringed whenever she thought about him—her estranged husband, Cain.

She was puzzled now more than ever, due to her change of fortune, regarding the exact, even the supposed, whereabouts of her husband. She must still regard him as that, until he be found and brought to trial and executed for the death of their child. He could, she reasoned, be in some foreign land and never again return to England. Or, being the hothead he was, he could have been killed in a brawl, or be hopelessly maimed and reduced to begging for a living. Or even living with some other woman: bigamously married to her. Why, they could even have a young family! Who was to know?

She held out her left hand, and stared at the third finger. Cain's ring she had thrown into Roxby Beck the morning she'd left Staithes—and her 'term of imprisonment', as she now looked upon that part of her life. She had been wearing it when Tom arrived in the village and they'd made love. Although he had noted its absence he'd not questioned her unduly.

Dear Tom! He was so very considerate. He probably imagined his interest in her might place her in an awkward situation, or even threaten their relationship. But yet… he should know—be made aware of—well… everything. And she must be brave. When next he called, she would tell all.

Tom listened as Sarah told her story. Not pressing her in any way, or asking things she might have found difficult to explain, he sat holding her hand as she poured out her tale of woe. When she had finished there was a long silence, then he said in a low voice, "Sarah… what you've just said—it makes not the slightest difference to how I feel for you. I love you. And even if you are, as you say, 'married', I still want you for the rest of my life. We have no secrets now, but we have something between us that can be beautiful. We can share… everything. I want to be part of you—all of you. I love you so very, very much."

There were tears in his eyes as she took him in his arms. "Tom… love me. Love me now. Let's… on the hearth-rug, if you want. I just want you to… oh, come on!" And, feeling very bold, she started tearing his clothes off.

"It's a good job"—and the Whitby apothecary seemed no longer shy as he started undoing her dress—"it's a good job Duncan isn't with me, or we'd have to send him to count the chickens, or feed the geese, or…"

And mere words seemed no longer to apply.

"Now, there are still one or two things I need to ask you, Mrs Dacre… and because I am acting in my professional capacity I must refer to you in that style"—and Stanhope Langden paused. Like a sculptor moulding a mass of clay, his hands moved accordingly as he continued. "Mrs Dacre, you say that you have no idea of the whereabouts of your husband. Who is a wanted man—a murderer, no less?"

"That's correct."

"And his family, his father and brothers, live in Staithes?"

"Yes, it was where I lived... when we were married."

"And since his disappearance you have come into a substantial inheritance. You are now a woman of independent means. And have been befriended by Mr Metcalfe, and the two of you have formed a relationship, which under normal circumstances would lead to marriage... were it not for the fact that you are 'married' already?"

"That's about it," Tom replied, but reading the look in Stanhope's eyes he gave a quick, "I'm sorry—I'm interrupting. And it's not really—"

"Mr Metcalfe, I do understand your position. I know you to be a man of good character, a decent member of society. And I fully appreciate your desire to protect Mrs Dacre. Rest assured, I shall do all that is within my power to bring this state of affairs to a satisfactory conclusion.

"There are," and he paused for effect (a familiar trick of his) "...*ways* of dealing with this. And I know the ideal man who can make discrete enquiries without drawing attention to himself, or the situation. But in the meantime, Mrs Dacre... might I enquire, and without in any way wishing to pry, about how you are coping with your new financial situation? If you have not already done so, might I suggest you engage an actuary to oversee all income from, and expenditure on, your various properties."

"An *actuary?*"

"He will, in simple terms, balance your books. There are those who might otherwise take advantage of you. All monies generated, profits from farm stock, rents and the like, will be accounted for. He would also oversee and advise on any investments you make in the future. It's something to consider."

Tom nodded in agreement.

"Then... there is an actuary I can personally recommend. Lives in Pickering, or as near as makes no difference. I could ask him to call on you."

"Please do, and thank you so much, Mr Langden"—and Sarah was beginning to feel quite important. Her earlier shyness had disappeared. She had a newfound confidence, knowing she had Tom by her side. "A man of good character, a decent member of society"—was how Stanhope Langden had described him. She could want for nothing more, and walked into the street with her head held high.

Scarcely had they left, than the man-of-the-law abruptly bellowed, "Jackson—Jackson—where the hell are you?"

"Here, Mr Langden, Sir."

"Jackson... I want you to walk down to the quay, where you'll probably find, or see somebody who knows the whereabouts of, that blackguard Malahide O'Connor. Since being disgraced and dismissed from his post as Preventative Officer he'll be more than grateful for anything anyone might care to throw him, as long as there's money in it at the end of the day. I want to see him: I have a job for him."

Sarah, now free of the confines of Low Clough Farm, and with both Tom and Duncan suggesting this-and-that (and pretending to take note of their suggestions), took stock of the garden which surrounded what was to be her new home. On the outskirts of the town, and with only one neighbour, here she could (she felt) be reasonably happy until such time as she and Tom could be... But that was in the future, and until they heard something definite from Stanhope Langden, then the two of them must appear to lead independent lives. She would, she supposed, miss having lambs in the fields and chickens scratching outside her door, but within the high-walled garden perhaps... but she dismissed the idea—a flock of geese would indiscriminately eat the flowers along with the weeds. She stared at clumps of purple *Aubretia* with stray daffodils growing through them, at a fruit tree coming into blossom, an overgrown lilac, an asparagus bed and beside it a rampant border of parsley. She'd be busy for months! Then she suddenly remembered—she could afford a gardener!

"And even peach trees against the wall," Tom was saying, "or a fig tree."

"We could have both."

"And strawberries," Duncan added. "I like strawberries."

"Then we'll have a strawberry bed as well. Now, do you gentleman have any further suggestions? If not, then we'll go inside and I'll get us something to eat. I've bought some gingerbread, I know Duncan likes it."

"You're spoiling him."

"Not at all. This young man deserves—and he can have... anything he wants," and Sarah put her arm round his shoulder. "Now, come on, the two of you. I'll show you the rest of the house when we've had a bite to eat."

Minutes later, as Duncan licked his now sticky fingers, he suddenly said, "when Leah and Ashley get married, you could come and live with us."

"...Well...!"

"Or we could come and live with you."

"Sarah might not want to live with us..."

"Well... I think we'd like to live with her!"

The two lovers grinned. "Eat up your gingerbread," Tom said to Duncan.

"It's Sarah, isn't it? Allow me to introduce myself. I'm Lady Celia, your neighbour."

Sarah stared at the sprightly middle-aged woman with red hair and daubs of rouge on each cheek not quite level, her neck weighed down with rows of beads hanging over a once expensive but now shabby dress. The head was tilted forward, the right hand outstretched.

"I'm... pleased to meet you."

"And you must call on me, should you need anything—anything at all," and Lady Celia was already in the hallway and trying to find her bearings. She opened a door. "The drawing room, I think—oh lovely, it gets the morning sun. And tell me, Sarah dear, do you live here alone? I look after my nephew. He's... oh—it's a long story. His parents think of him as an embarrassment and have abandoned him, so to speak."

"How terrible."

"Indeed—and he is their only son and the heir-presumptive, and will, upon the death of my brother by the rules of agnostic succession inherit the title. He is now a mere Lord, but one day he will be an Earl."

Sarah stared in amazement. "I didn't realise I was living in such a select area."

"Oh, my dear, we're no different from anyone else—we all have 'things' in the family we like to keep hidden."

Sarah nodded in agreement. There was something about Lady Celia. She felt as if they had been friends for years.

"And I saw young... er... Duncan? Yes, that's right, that's his name, isn't it. From the apothecary. Yes, I saw Duncan in your garden a few days ago. Such a polite young boy, very nice."

"So is Tom," Sarah blurted out.

Lady Celia nodded. "Oh yes. And are the two of you... do you have an understanding?"

"Yes."

"I'm so very pleased for you. Tom Metcalfe is a fine young man—shall we have a glass of sherry or something?"

"Why not?"

Sarah opened a cabinet, and produced two glasses and a bottle.

"To celebrate our new friendship! And you must call on me one afternoon next week and meet my nephew. Bring Duncan with you. He and Lord Percival will get on famously."

The boy had an abnormally small chin and an unusually round face, an almond shape to the eyes caused by an upstanding fold of the eyelid, and a protruding tongue. He had shorter than average limbs for one of his age, and as he held his hand out, a single instead of double crease across his palms was evident.

"And this is my nephew, Lord Percival," and Lady Celia shook her head and gave a sigh. "The price of too much interbreeding, I'm afraid... But he loves living with his auntie, don't you."

"Yes." His voice in reply was like the rasp of a terrier.

"I pretend he's two years younger than he really is. " Lady Celia excused her nephew's shortcomings, "and he's really very bright—but as you can imagine, his parents with their society friends... and... well, need I say more? Now, do come in the two of you, tea's all ready."

"Scones"—Lord Percival rasped from the back of his throat, "we're having scones and raspberry jam."

"Now, you must look after Duncan," his aunt instructed him, "the two of you can sit next to one another, then after tea you can show him your toys, and the two of you can play."

Duncan was somewhat bemused, but at the same time polite toward his new friend, and nearing the end of the meal as the two were devouring chocolate cake the hostess had a sudden thought. "French lessons!"

Her guests turned toward her.

"Er... I was just... we have a tutor visiting us every alternate Thursday afternoon to give Percival French lessons... and he does seem to do better if he has someone to work alongside him. I don't suppose that you'd consider—but you'd have to ask Tom if he could spare him—and it wouldn't cost anything, because I'm paying anyway. Would you like to learn to speak a foreign language, Duncan?"

"Dunno."

"I'll mention it to Tom. Obviously I can't say yes or no, but... "

"Splendid. Now, do you two young gentlemen want to... go and play? But don't go near the bee-hives."

"—Or you get stung."

Lady Celia nodded to the now-Lord-but-at-some-point-to-be-Earl. "That's right, Percival. You are a clever boy, and no mistake."

"Having tea with a Lord, no less," Tom teased his brother, "my word, you *are* moving up in the world."

"And Lady Celia suggested… that he might like to join Lord Percival for French lessons."

"By gum lad, tha's arrived," and Tom gave him an affectionate cuddle. "If you want to learn a fancy foreign language then you can. Duncan, you can have anything you want."

Chapter 15

The more Tom looked for tell-tale clues that all was not well, the more obsessed he became, so that when there were no customers he would just stand and stare, wanting to say something, but at the same time not in any way aggravate the situation.

Finally he decided that the two of them should have a short holiday. Away from Whitby, on their own, he hoped that Duncan would tell him just what was troubling him.

"How's about… we board the coach tomorrow morning and have a few days in Scarborough?"

Duncan seemed quite unmoved at such a suggestion, and merely nodded his head in agreement.

"Then we'll ask Leah to pack a change of clothes for us… and tomorrow morning we'll be away."

"But who'll look after the shop?"

"Oh, Leah will be all right on her own, or we could even ask Ashley to keep her company. Now, let's make a list of the things we'll need to take with us—we'll want lots of money, won't we."

The lad nodded, but kept a wedge-bone expression until Tom started tickling his ribs. "Cheer up, what's the matter?"

"Nothing."

"Good. Shall we nibble some chocolate?"

"Mmm."

"Are you two gentlemen all right?" Leah, back from her morning shopping had with her loaves of freshly baked bread, and sitting on top of her basket something looking like a sponge cake.

"We've been talking about the Scarborough trip, and Duncan's going to come with me to keep me company."

"That's nice."

"And if… er… Mrs Dalgleish should come in wanting anything you're 'doubtful' about—then we don't have it."

"I know what you mean."

"Cough linctus and the like will be fine. Leeches, no—and if she should ask for a cure for impotency in elderly sea-captains, any 'mercury' treatments or the like, then tell her we're clean out of them."

"She certainly making her mark on the town. Everybody seems to know her, or know *of* her."

"I'm not surprised."

"Never has there been such an abundance of dashing young soldiers in Whitby," Leah mused. "Their scarlet uniforms quite bring the town to life."

"Really? I do hope they're going to remain healthy. If they catch something unpleasant they'll need more than stomach bitters or worm syrup—now, Duncan, do you want to help Leah put the shopping away, and then she'll sort some clothes out for you to take with us."

The lad nodded, Tom thought about Scarborough, customers came and went, the Town Hall clock struck the hour, Ashley called, and was invited to stay for lunch—the day promised to be like any other.

Travelling to Scarborough was an adventure, not only to Duncan, but also for Tom, as indeed, was the town itself when they embarked at the coaching inn.

" Now," Tom asked, "where shall we go first? What would you like to see?"

"Let's go and walk on the sands."

"But we can do that in Whitby."

"… Well, it'll be different here," Duncan reasoned.

"All right then. But we'll first get to our room where we can freshen up and leave our things."

The room had a huge four-poster, and on a marble stand-stand stood a blue and white jug and bowl beside which were white towels, and the window had a view onto a busy street below and in the distance, a ruined castle. Nodding toward it, Tom informed his adopted sibling, "King Richard the Third is said to have been the last King of England to have stayed there, we can take a walk round the ruins later, if you like."

"Mmm. You know lots of things don't you, Tom."

"Not really. When you're grown up you'll know much more—after all, you already know lots and lots about herbs and things."

"Yes, but you've taught me all that."

"Just as uncle Nathan taught me. This 'special' knowledge we have to hand on—but yet keep secret, if you follow my meaning."

"Yes. I wouldn't tell anything to… Lord Percival," then Duncan added, " still, I don't suppose it would make a lot of difference if I did."

"No, but the lad's kind, and quite harmless."

"Perhaps you could make up a bottle of syrup, or linctus… to make him like other boys."

Tom shook his head. "If only."

"But there must be something," Duncan insisted, "for you always tell me that for every ailment and condition, there is a herb that can cure it."

"I'm sure there is—it's just a question of discovering it. Now let's start exploring Scarborough. The sands or the castle?"

Duncan looked out of the window. He'd changed his mind. "The castle!"

Several days later, and feeling very energetic and bold, the two of them decided that instead of riding, they would walk the thirty or so miles to Whitby. The journey becoming a game of testing Duncan's knowledge of the plants, such as they came upon.

"Cuckoo pint," Duncan straightway named two pale green leaves sprouting among the hawthorn hedge.

"And what other names does it have?"

"Lords and Ladies—and when it gets its berries, Naked Boys"—and Duncan giggled.

"… And the next, young man… er… what's this clump?"

"Foxglove leaves."

"And when they're small like these are, what do they remind you of?"

Duncan stared. "Dunno."

"Sage leaves. Look, they have the same dull green colour, and sort of whiteish fur—but there the similarity ends. Because foxgloves do—what?"

Duncan considered. "Cause the heart to beat in an irregular pattern and slow it down—until it stops altogether."

"You're absolutely right. Now, in that garden, see… the plant with the tall blue spikes?"

"Monkshood. It causes a burning feeling and tingling in the mouth, and it can also kill you."

Tom nodded, then added for good measure, "It's other name is Wolfsbane, because it was used to kill wolves, and ancient warriors used it to poison the water supply to kill their enemies. There are other things in this garden that are poisonous, lets see… "

"Laburnum," Duncan pointed to the tree already hung with as yet unopened flowers—and rhododendron. They're poisonous, aren't they?"

"Mmm—you really do know a great deal, don't you."

"Not so much as you."

"Well, Duncan, uncle Nathan taught me all I know, just as I'm teaching you. Because…" and Tom paused. "Because," he began again, "when I get too old for it, I shall want you to be in charge of the shop, and someday it will be yours. You've become a very special part of our lives, and I know something's bothering you, and that worries me. Now, what's the matter?"

Suddenly Duncan looked away and started kicking stones.

"Come on, we don't have secrets."

"Well," he finally managed, "when Leah gets married... and if you and Sarah..."

"Yes?"

"...You won't want me in the way, will you?" and Duncan seemed close to tears. "You see, Ashley and Leah wouldn't want me to live with them... and..."

"Here—what's all this silly talk about? You're my brother, part of me. You like Sarah, don't you?"

"Mmm."

"Well then—is this why you've been so quiet, these last few days? And here's me thinking you'd been in another fight with young Langden and burst his nose again."

"Oh him? He's just fat and stupid."

"Nor does he have a mate who's the son of an Earl. By gum, lad, but you're going places! Now, is everything all right between us?"

Duncan nodded, although still close to tears.

"Then give me a hug, and we'll get a bite to eat at the next place we see. We do love you, you know. All of us."

They returned home late that evening, exhausted, but suddenly revived by the feverish activity in the vicinity of the quayside as the dreaded impress-men were hounding men and boys to enlist them in His Majesty's Navy. There were skirmishes along Baxtergate, and the men darted this way and that between the many alleys and ghauts to evade capture.

One officer was thrown over the bridge, guns rang out—and from nowhere appeared an army of women who had taken it upon themselves to deal with this latest attack on the town's menfolk. Armed with sticks and stones, one woman even with a sabre, they were a formidable force. A further two impress officers suffered serious injuries before the Whitby men reached comparative safety as they raced toward Upgang and the woods near Cock Mill.

Chapter 16

Acting upon Stanhope's earlier advice, Sarah's finances were now in the hands of one Jabez Trotwood, an actuary who had grown so successful that no longer did he have to advertise his services but would take new clients only on personal recommendation. And Sarah, having placed the day to day running of the farms in the hands of an agent, now needed only find a suitable tenant for Far Clough and her worries in that department would be at an end.

They had booked rooms at the *Fox and Partridge* (on the advice of her land agent) well in advance of the event, and when they saw the crowds already assembling for the Hiring Fair, both realised the good sense of John Carlow's words, for all the farming community in the entire county and beyond were, it seemed, converging or about to converge on this village.

At first light, on the day of the fair proper, workers were gathering in the streets, proudly displaying the tools of their trade. Dairy-maids, carrying a milking stool or a pail, shepherds with their crooks, cowmen with wisps of straw stuck in their hats, housemaids with a broom or a mop. Tradesmen (and women) seemed to encompass every aspect of every possible trade or profession. A cook had with her a wooden spoon, a gardener a spade, thatchers carried bundles of straw, there was a blacksmith with a horseshoe in his hat, while a bailiff carried a lanthorn.

Sarah gazed, remembering a similar scene several years previously when, with her father, she had paraded as these workers were now doing. A fateful day, one that seemed destined to haunt her for the rest of her life. But she must put those feelings aside, she was with Tom, and the world was now a wonderful place.

Along with those seeking employment was the only-to-be-expected entourage of horse dealers, fortune tellers, card tricksters, men selling pretty trinkets, generously proportioned women selling mutton pies and toffee, a man selling quails eggs. There was a stall selling gingerbread, cordials and various sweetmeats, another with skeins of wool died in all manner of colours. There was a woman making (and selling) lace, her bobbins swirling round her fingers, dogs were prancing as the smell of pease pudding assailed their nostrils, a man with a fiddle was trying to made himself heard, and two men walking on stilts were attracting a crowd of onlookers.

Tom and Sarah moved through all this with the firm determination, besides enjoying the entertainment and euphoria, at the end of the day to have secured a new tenant for Far Clough Farm.

"And I have with me a contract drawn up by my agent, which you should read before we seal the bargain with the customary shilling"—and Sarah took from her bag a large envelope which she handed to the husband and wife for their perusal. "It's good arable land, thirty acres or thereabouts, and I do own the adjoining ten acre field, should you—"

"John Carlow's your agent, then?"

"Do you know him?"

Husband and wife nodded. "As straight as they come, is John Carlow," the man replied. "He's a fair bloke, I'll say that for him. Doesn't stand fools, but nor does he use fancy words or play dirty tricks." The couple looked at one another and nodded. "We'd like to take on Far Clough Farm, Miss."

Events seemed, for Leah Metcalfe, to have come to a sudden halt.

The house, which should have been ready months ago, still needed to be decorated, the elaborate plaster stucco ceilings and friezes were waiting for their several coats of paint, floorboards were pleading to be stained and polished, walls that she longed to see covered in pictures and mirrors were still devoid of these things, and the windows with no drapes seemed signs of poverty. Ashley had taken temporary premises as his consulting rooms, and seemed to have spent all his energy and enthusiasm furnishing these to his liking at the expense of what she viewed much more important: their new home.

And—and she tried not to feel a pang of jealousy, her brother was now (and it had happened all so quickly) head-over-heels in love with this Sarah woman, who had suddenly arrived upon the Whitby scene. It was less than three months—three months, and his world was completely topsy-turvy. If he were not staying with her all night then he was mooning all day like a lovesick calf—and Whitby knew, oh yes, all Whitby knew what was going on. They really had no shame, either of them. No shame at all.

There was a sharp wind coming from the sea and a blue cloudless sky, and Tom Metcalfe was suddenly the age of the lad beside him as he and Duncan stood watching the yearly Whitby Ascension Day ritual, the planting of the Penny Hedge. As the men arrived carrying the bundles of hazel stakes, Duncan urged his way forward to get a better view while Tom once again related the tale of the three men who killed a religious hermit as he was trying to protect the wild boar they were hunting. The abbot of Whitby was sent for, who finally condescended to forgive the men on condition that they, and their descendants, each year on Ascension Day, did penance by weaving a short hedge of hazel stakes to be planted on the east side of the harbour, which must stand intact and upright for three tides.

Breaking into his tale Duncan suddenly asked, "then why is it called a 'penny hedge'—why not a hazel hedge?"

"Because there was also a stipulation that the wood had to be cut from Eskdaleside with a knife costing a penny."

"You know everything about everything, don't you."

"Just about," Tom smirked, "and I also know we'll have to race back to Church Street when the ceremony's over, or Leah will think we're leaving her to do all the work."

Suddenly a horn was sounded to signify that the planting was complete, and the words *"Out on thee!"* rang out three times. The crowd began to disperse.

It was all over until next Ascension Eve. Another Whitby tradition—yet Duncan needed to know about all these things. They were part of the town, and he was quickly becoming part of it.

"We are doomed to spinsterhood," Constance Langden commiserated with her friend on hearing of yet another postponement to what was supposed to be the happiest day in a woman's life, while Leah, very near to tears nodded in agreement. "Why, oh why did we fall in love with ship's surgeons," Constance asked, "when we could have had the pick of all the eligible young men in Whitby—all of Yorkshire, even?"

She paused to look in the mirror, struck up a pose, then continued, "Young men with prospects—titles, even—who'd worship the ground we walked on."

"And with blond hair falling over their forehead?" Leah asked hopefully, thinking of Ashley.

"Absolutely."

"And kind and gentle? With lovely hands?"

Constance nodded. "And they'd always be smiling, and attentive to our needs."

"And buy us presents?"

"And be so proud to show us off to Society. Glittering balls, the theatre, soirées, literary circles and the like."

"But would they be willing to offer marriage?"

"Probably not—but we'd be kept in a very grand manner," and their earlier resentment and frustration hving been played out, the two women threw themselves into each other's arms and burst into uncontrollable laughter,

"Men!"

"Who needs them?"

"…We do," they chorused.

"Unless, of course we were to become nuns."

"Where?" and Leah stared wide eyed. "How would we set about it?"

"Well, I understand that Mrs Dalgleish runs a 'nunnery' of sorts. She always has some poor girl who is 'for marriage and not for pleasure'—at least, not until the wedding night."

"Really?"

"Oh yes, but"—and Constance paused, as though to collect her thoughts. Then she began, "there's a nunnery at York—though of course, we'd need to change our religion and become Roman Catholics."

"Oh."

It was a bitter joke—and Leah didn't laugh. Even to countenance such a possibility had unseated the Prime Minister three years earlier.

"You don't appear to be in love with the idea."

"I'd rather be married—to Ashley!"

"Yes, I suppose my brother is the most handsome man in Whitby—but I'm only saying that because Lynton's at sea again."

"Of course."

"And when he leaves His Majesty's Navy and comes to live with me and Papa? Well then, my much-loved brother will have competition." Then, suddenly serious, Constance sighed. "But that's in the distant future, isn't it. Why, my Lynton could be at sea for months, years even—who can tell?"

"And all the while Ashley is so adamant that Lynton should be at his side when we're married. He so wants him to be his man, and given a place of honour."

"And they do say that 'one wedding makes another' which leads me to enquire about Tom and this… this Sarah woman."

Leah shook her head. "Something of a mystery. How exactly he knew her before she first came into the shop he never said, and I think even Duncan knows more than me. But of course, he and Tom really are like brothers these days, sharing secrets and full of boyish tricks. Tom often wakens up to find Duncan snuggled up to him trying to get warm, and they think its fun teasing me when I ask about the farm at Sleights."

"She's a farmer's daughter?"

"A woman of means—for she owns several farms in the area, together with various properties and—"

"And is she beautiful?"

Leah paused. "She's… yes, I think she is, in her own way. She's not like us, but… well, she's not afraid of hard work, and she's polite… and… yes—she's very nice."

"I used to think when we were children… that me and Tom would be sweethearts… and you and Ashley, of course, and that we'd all sort of get married and live happily ever after."

"Mmm."

"If only—yet I sometimes feel that this 'waiting for marriage' is a life-long project, like a massive medieval wall hanging, and we work at it relentlessly, year after year, sometimes until the day we die. We have the threads between our fingers, yet we're just repeating the same pattern, we can't break into anything new. Leah, do you think I'll be working on this tapestry until I die?"

Constance waited for an answer. And for once in her life, Leah was stuck for words.

Late spring turned into early summer and Stanhope Langden (as had now become his yearly ritual) went to Harrogate to 'take the waters'. The smell from the lant ships moored out at sea became close to unbearable when combined with the putrefying odour from the many yards and alleys with their unemptied privvies. There was also the perpetual stink of fish and the haze of bluebottles which their discarded innards attracted. All these things, combined with the unwholesome perfumes from the quayside, convinced Mrs Dalgleish that it was time to move herself and her entourage to London, 'for the season'.

Yet there was one man who, acting upon a half-tale he'd been told when he was earlier in Staithes, moved among these obnoxious, festering harbourside fumes with the cunning of a sewer rat.

Malahide O'Connor.

From the sailors' whores to Old Peg-leg, who hobbled about the town and missed nothing, Malahide made it known that he was searching for a man with a purple right hand. The man was in grave danger and should contact the former Preventative Officer with all due speed, as he had certain information for him. The Irishman, having woven a net of intrigue, would now let the hunted track down the hunter. The trap was baited: Malahide O'Connor must now wait for Cain Dacre to approach him.

Cain Dacre was now not only a man with a mark—he was also a marked man!

He was becoming a busy man, his services in great demand. And to cope with this success Ashley Langden now engaged an assistant. A pimply-faced young man with an obsession for cleanliness, and a somewhat misplaced notion that a thorough examination of the patient's private parts was absolutely essential before any surgery could be so much as contemplated. On his first morning (and with great delight) he helped examine a somewhat shy young man who was having 'marital problems'.

"A simple operation," Ashley assured the patient. "It should have been done years ago. Shall we say… Friday of next week?"

Anxious to be free of any further manipulations by the assistant and the discomfort this was producing, the young man immediately agreed, dressed hurriedly and departed. Tobias washed his hands yet again, and later that morning helped examine a man with a gumboil, and not, as the patient had feared, a manifestation of the dreaded pox. Only when Ashley shook his head did he refrain from removing the patient's breeches to investigate what was being hidden.

The afternoon was busy cupping and blooding, and Ashley was reminded of reading somewhere about 'each bloody second dripping into the receptacle of time' and thought how very profound that was. Tobias was busy removing stitches from an arm that had earlier been in a fight, then the two of them needed to convince an unfrocked clergyman who was still suffering as a result of his 'sinful lusts of the flesh' that he must consult a doctor in regard to his worsening condition.

"Temptation—temptation is everywhere!" The no-longer man of the cloth wailed. "On the streets, and in taverns—especially such places of ill-repute, where young serving girls lure men to their rooms, and for only pence—yes, mere pence, gentleman, exhibit their nakedness to inflame a man's passions. While late at night the harlots of Zion shamelessly parade the streets—why, the very air is charged with wickedness! These painted Jezebels openly ply their trade, luring and seducing men with their lascivious smiles and cheap pefume… Oh—the flesh is weak, gentlemen, the flesh is weak. We are all sinners, and the wages of sin are—"

"A dose of clap," Ashley mouthed the words to Tobias.

"…Eternal fire and damnation," the rhetoric continued, " and there are other temptations. Sodomy, self-abuse in the form of masturbation, and other more unspeakable fornications. Incest, bestiality, bondage, flagellation, carnal knowledge *per rectum*—and so very many other degrading sexual deviations one could mention and elaborate upon. Oh, the weakness of men when tempted by the female of the species! And the wickedness of women who flaunt their"—and he shook his head in despair. " Man that is born of woman... oh—gentlemen, the temptations of the flesh! The painted lips of the harlot—the quayside fleshpots where the very air is putrefied with the wickedness and wantonness of lewd, sexual desires—the fruits of sin contaminating our very thoughts. Satan's harvest surely, being for everlasting flames."

Ashley noticed a glazed look in the gentleman's eyes as he continued, "And London? Well, it would seem to me a very cesspit of impurity, with temptresses openly plying their trade around Covent Garden and Charing Cross—St Martin's-in-the-Fields, why—there are even shameful establishments known as Molly Houses where men perform unnatural acts with each other, the very air putrefied with the stench of carnal lust."

"Really?"

The ecclesiastical breathing became laboured, as he shook his head in despair. "It is a wicked world—why, only days ago a young woman called on me, begging me for spiritual guidance and corrective treatment, resulting in my having to bring my hand down heavily across her bare buttocks as I proceeded to give her a good spanking. She had strong thighs, gentlemen, but she left my bed with a subdued spirit... and a shilling in her purse for services rendered."

It was the first of the month, the day when Ashley, aided by Tobias, held court at the hospital, giving their services free (but at the same time considerably enhancing the surgeon's quickly growing reputation). The first patient of the morning, clad in nothing but his wig, was already on the operating table. Knees up in the air, wrists bound to his ankles, he would be held in that position by two strong porters throughout the entire operation. Quite unable to move, he was at the mercy of the surgeon and his assistant.

"If you've never seen a lithotomy done before, don't faint," Ashley warned his assistant, as he moved toward the patient, trussed up like a chicken ready for the oven. He picked up his knife, mentally balancing it between his fingers, as he weighed up the patients chances of survival, and his own success—but now was not the time to speculate on such matters. On his sleeve were various needles, threaded and ready for use. Tobias was also ready as he pushed the oiled catheter into the urethra. After much groaning from the patient, Tobias indicated that he had located the stone. There was a cutting silence, followed by deafening screams, as Ashley swiftly made his incision. Then working by touch, fingers holding the wound apart, right hand catching up the gorgeret, then the forceps, the stone was withdrawn from the bladder. Tobias attended to the sutures as Ashley held up the calculus in his fingers.

The patient was back in the land of the living. His breathing was somewhat erratic, but he nevertheless managed a glass of brandy.

Ashley looked at the bloodied hands of his helper. His face was ashen: he looked in worse condition than the patient.

Chapter 17

The ensuing weeks saw what Leah hopefully took to be signs that the wedding was coming closer, as the workmen and decorators completed their work on the house in Bagdale, and she and Ashley were able to buy furniture to help transform the mere "house" into a home.

Her husband-to-be nodded in approval as Leah held Italian brocades for turning into drapes and curtains before him for his opinion. But he left the choice of furniture for the drawing room entirely to her: chandeliers with cascading cut glass prisms, elegant pier glass mirrors, luxurious rugs, a salon suite—and there was the bedroom!

Feeling very bold, she held his hand as they looked at big four-poster beds, and Leah imagined her wedding night. When the two of them would be alone... and more than likely—well, certainly—*that* would happen. What, or *how* exactly, was still something of a mystery, but she would cope, as just every other bride did. And if she had any doubts? Well, she supposed, she could always ask Sarah. For any earlier distance between them had now vanished... and she needed to look to the future.

For when she and Ashley were wed, Tom would have uncle Nathan and also Duncan to cope with on his own, and there would be the shop, and the customers. For she herself would have a husband to care for and a home to organise and run. Ashley would need a wife who could entertain in the grand manner, and there would also be babies and things.

He gave her hand a squeeze. "What are you thinking?"

"Ashley!"—and she suddenly giggled, "What a silly thing to ask when we're looking at beds."

"Oh, my dear, just wait until our wedding night!" And their smiles turned to wicked, shameless laughter.

She was dressed in scarlet—the latest London fashion—the wig was elaborately coiffured and further trimmed with feathers, and with blue-and-gold-liveried Xavier in attendance Mrs Dalgleish, despite her age (and profession) cut quite a figure. "Mr Langden," she called again to Ashley, "oh, Mr Langden, how nice—how very nice—to see you."

"Ma-am."

"Please, call me Gloriana—for I feel we are old friends. And without further pleasantries I must tell you my good news. I have successfully arranged a splendid future for little Amy, and any day now she will be known as The Right Honourable, the Countess of… she's to marry an Earl. What do you think of that, then?"

"I hope she'll be very happy."

"She'll certainly be well cared for. And Camille has also done well for herself, for she's now under the protection of a banker and is being kept in a very grand manner. She has a house in Chandos Street, and also has her own maid."

"Very good."

"But Bernice has returned to Whitby with me, and also two young girls from Covent Garden. There's Sally, a shy little creature who has only recently been deflowered, and is now available for *considerate* young men (such as yourself)—and then there's Audrey, my latest merchandise. She's noted not only for her desire (indeed, with her it is a vocation—the very essence of her being—to please men) but also for her sparkling wit. And she claims she has never yet been blessed with a *satisfying* meal of manhood… and so, Mr Langden, should you think you could meet her desires and be man enough to 'rise to the occasion' so to speak, then Audrey will look forward to being of service to you. She has an amorous constitution and, when in the arms of an equally lewd partner, never wishes to fall asleep. Before coming under my protection she was in a house in Tavistock Row, where she offered a nightly lodging of two guineas, half to be refunded if the man satisfied her—and many a young Buck has done that! She has only been known to decline one gentleman throughout her career. A queer cull he was, no less, so her refusal was only to be expected.

"Dear little Audrey would nightly sacrifice herself on the altar of Venus, and since she has become such a convert to love and libertinism, well—I fear Whitby might seem but a trifle to her. Still, when her presence here becomes known, she should have no shortage of suitors… and there'll doubtless be an abundance of military uniforms in the vicinity of our premises!"

Ashley looked around anxiously, lest anyone should imagine he was becoming too familiar with the woman.

Abruptly she waved her hand. "It is so—*so*—very different from London. The rides in the park, where my girls could display themselves, the boxes at the theatres—the London society!"

"Yet you've returned."

"Indeed—and, Mr Langden, I do hope you'll be able to call on me tomorrow evening. For after an indulgent few weeks in the capital, seeming to absolutely gorge myself—for I visited every London restaurant of note, and ate all manner of things bad for the figure and one's wellbeing, I shall need blooding. A full twelve ounces—then I shall be as pale as a lily, without recourse to the white lead for my face. Blooding is nature's best cosmetic."

"Then I shall call on you tomorrow evening—with my assistant Tobias." Ashley decided to tease her. "He's very young… and I believe him to be quite inexperienced. You must treat him gently."

And Mrs Dalgleish gave a knowing nod.

Having returned from Harrogate fortified and invigorated, and with the energy and (unfortunately for his waistline) the appetite of six men, Stanhope Langden stared enviously (albeit briefly) at the lean figure in front of him. There was simply no justice in the world!

"Well," he barked—his "professional" manner being reserved for clients, "what has your snooping so far unearthed?"

"Indeed, Mr Langden, I'm thinking you'll be—"

"And don't wipe snot all over your sleeve when you're in my office."

"Sorry, Mr Langden—to be sure, er… er… "

"Well, come on, man. Do you have any news concerning Cain Dacre?"

Malahide O'Connor pursed his lips, paused for effect, then staring straight ahead said simply, "I'll not be about wasting my time looking for Cain Dacre…"

"Whyever not…?"

"Because he will be looking for me."

As Malahide told his tale, the man-of-the-law seemed to mellow, almost warm, toward the Irishman. He thought the fellow was either very clever, or unbelievably stupid, for placing himself in such a dangerous situation for the cause.

"So… when—*if*—Cain Dacre should in any way contact you, what will you do?"

"I'll be letting you know the moment he does, Mr Langden, Sir—that I will."

"But supposing he's… oh, let's say… made a new life for himself the other side of the world—or is even dead?"

"Then he'll not be troubling us at all, at all."

Stanhope considered. There was a certain sense in the man's words—but it still left the crucial question unanswered.

Where *was* Cain Dacre?

The apothecary's preparation room was heavy with the scent of elderflowers spread out on tables to dry before being stored for winter use.

And, because of her friendship with Sarah, Lady Celia had promised bunches of lavender from her garden, together with sprays of southernwood and also whatever Tom and Duncan felt might be beneficial to their business. Lady Celia's herb garden, thanks to many years of nurturing, was now an apothecary's paradise. Tom moved from herb to herb, naming and explaining the properties of each plant to Duncan, who marvelled at his tutor.

"And even in the main garden there are lots of flowers with medicinal properties. The deep red rose petals—for the heart—and mallow for stomach ulcers, and the flowers can even be used as a compress for abscesses and minor burns... and this is—?" He touched the clump of flowers in front of him.

"Valerian," Duncan replied. "It makes you drowsy."

"It does indeed."

"Sarah says"—and Duncan's thoughts were suddenly far away from herbs and the like—"that we might call at Far Clough... because they'll be haymaking."

"And so...?"

"She says we can take a pic-nic"—and he tried to make it sound even more tempting—"and Lord Percival might even come with us..."

Tom grinned. "...Well, it's all arranged then. You like Sarah, don't you. The two of you get on well together."

"Mmm. She's nice. And she's going to bake all sorts of things—and we can even take bottles of raspberry cordial."

"Well, we'll have to ask Leah if she can manage without us before we decide anything definite..."

Abruptly Duncan changed the topic. "Leah's very worried about her wedding, isn't she."

"Well... " and Tom tried to make light of his sister's predicament, "she's hoping to fix the date soon—but Ashley's a very busy man... and..."

"He's not as nice as you."

"Hey, come on! He's all right."

"Yes—but I'd rather have you for my brother."

Tom put his arm round him. On occasions words were quite superfluous.

"A white silk, with bunches of pale blue forget-me-nots. What do you think?"

"It sounds lovely," Constance enthused, "and you could carry a posy of blue-and-white flowers—and with blue-and-white ribbons in your hair."

"I'd never thought of that—or a blue-and-white bonnet, even."

"And... when is it to be, Leah?"

"Well, the house is ready—or will be, by the end of the month. The decorators have moved out, the furniture, or most of it has arrived, the curtains are at the windows. Ashley has ordered coal and logs for the fires, the men are to lay the carpets any day... we need things like cutlery and crockery—and bed linen, and towels and... oh—Constance, isn't it exciting."

"Mmm," and her friend felt a twinge of jealousy. Yet again she thought: life seemed unfair to her, with Lynton so far away.

"And not only *when*—we also have to decide *where*. There's the Silver Street Chapel, or the one in Flowergate—"

"Or the West Cliff Congregational." Constance capped her friend's merry jest.

"Or, of course, St Mary's next to the Abbey. What do you think, Constance? Which one would you choose?"

"St Mary's, without a doubt."

"Then that's where it will be. I wish—I used to imagine—that we'd have a double wedding: me and Ashley—and you and Lynton."

Her friend sighed. "If only, Leah... if only...!"

On being recognised by the new tenants of Far Clough, Alice-Anne, the farmer's wife, somewhat shyly invited Tom and Sarah and their charges to a bread-and-cheese lunch in the hayfield.

"We've brought something with us we could all share," said Sarah. "Come on, Alice-Anne, I'll give you a hand," and the two women went to prepare the mid-day meal. Sarah looked round the kitchen, and memories came flooding back, Alice-Anne took bottles of home-made cider from the well and wrapped them in a cloth, then frantically searched for something to drink from. "We don't usually have company," was her excuse for her somewhat strange collection of drinking vessels.

"It's all right, really it is. After all, we did drop-in unannounced"—and then Sarah noticed a roundness about the farmer's wife. "When the baby due?"

"December, I'm thinking."

"And is the farm getting to be hard work?"

"Oh!"—and Alice-Anne pulled a face, "you know what it's like. It's all right for the menfolk. They have their fun, and... How about you and your young man? Are you planning to wed?"

"Anything's possible." Sarah tried to make light of the question, but it was something she asked herself, every night, without coming to any sort of conclusion.

"And the two young lads?"

"Oh, Duncan is Tom's darling brother—and as for Lord Percival... I suppose you'll know, or at least have heard of, Lady Celia? She's well-known in these parts. She's my neighbour—and Lord Percival is her nephew. They live together in Whitby, well away from the bustle of London."

"Oh, I see..."

"And he's... well, he's a very kind boy. And he's... oh, it's not the lad's fault—he's just the unfortunate result of cousins repeatedly marrying cousins. Too much interbreeding can have unfortunate consequences, as you'll know only too well, being a farmer's wife."

"We need to keep changing the bull."

"Exactly."

Back in the field the two boys were having fun as they romped in the hay. But at the end of the afternoon Duncan had arms and neck burning from the sun—and Lord Percival's face was redder than usual. As they bid their visitors farewell they were invited to the next big event in the farming calendar: the harvest supper, to be held after the last sheaf of corn had been gathered-in.

"We'll be there, never fear"—and Sarah seemed extraordinarily happy as they made their way back to Whitby.

"You don't miss Far Clough, do you?"

She considered that, then shook her head. "I much prefer the life I have now... and the future it could hold."

"Things will work out, you know."

"I know, Tom. And I do love you."

"And I love you... But I have to get Duncan home tonight. Or else I'd..."

Sarah nodded. "I do understand, and it's no problem. You might wish to call tomorrow evening...?"

He took her hand. "I might wish to do just that."

But the events of the following morning were so unexpected that the entire household was thrown into a state of utter confusion, so utterly unprepared were they for the eventuality.

He had been fine, showing no sign of illness or anything untoward, and Tom and Leah assumed that he was having a lie-in. The breakfast things were being cleared away as Hannah the daily help arrived and began her usual chores. The hands moved to half past nine, then when the clock struck ten and there was still no sign of uncle Nathan, Tom went to his room. He seemed still asleep.

Then Tom moved to wake him, and some seconds later called out for Leah.

"Yes?"

"Leah, he's dead." And brother and sister gazed down at the old man who had been so kind to them—so very kind.

Leah stared incredulously. Her breathing became laboured and she suddenly burst into tears as she threw her arms around her brother. "Oh Tom, what shall we do?" she finally managed between her sobbing. "What shall we do?"

"Best… start making arrangements. I'm all-at-sea, just as you are. We must tell Hannah and Duncan… and then… er, I'd best get him ready and laid-out… and see about a coffin, and all that."

"And we must close the shop, and put a notice in the window. *Closed, due to family bereavement.*"

"Aye"—and Tom looked again at the lifeless body. "Poor uncle Nathan."

Drapes and shutters were drawn, heavy black crêpe fastened to the doorknocker, a vase of lilies placed in the shop window and mantelpiece, picture frames and mirrors were draped in black. Between the day of his death and the actual funeral the entire population of Whitby, or so it seemed, called to pay their respects to the kindly old man, who had so unexpectedly been called to his maker, and was now laid-out in a shroud of pale blue silk, in a room smelling of sandalwood and myrrh.

The morning of the funeral dawned, the sun spilled over the sea, seagulls screamed, the populace of Whitby went about their business. After a hurried breakfast Tom and Duncan changed into their mourning attire and Leah was again visited by Ashley, who was so very concerned for her welfare.

Hannah (who since the uncle's death had practically taken up residence) was on-hand to make drinks and deal with the eternal washing-up of mugs and plates. People were beginning to arrive for the eleven o'clock service at St Mary's. Sarah, painful thoughts of her father's recent death surfacing. Constance, with Stanhope at her side—a man who so often in the course of his business had to appear as such—seemed quite unaffected, as the conventional scenario began to unfold.

A local shopkeeper was busy fitting mourners and friends for gloves and armbands. Wine and funeral biscuits were being offered, and in return condolences to the family. The man-of-the-law glanced round the room. It was a good turn-out!

Shopkeepers, the tea merchant from a few doors further along the street, the local tailor, wine-and-spirit merchant, cabinet maker and joiner, men from the boatyard, a Whitby ship owner and… and he suddenly noticed Lady Celia in close conversation with his client, Sarah Dacre. The funeral was even attracting the local aristocracy.

Outside the apothecary shop, horses with plumes of ostrich feathers were impatiently prancing, the funeral hearse waiting to begin its journey along Church Street to the hundred-and-ninety-nine steps leading to the abbey and St Mary's. A lot of steps for a man of Stanhope's proportions: he needed another glass of sustenance, for the procession was about to begin.

Leah, supported by Tom and Duncan and followed by close friends (for it appeared that the deceased had no other family) began to form up outside in the street. Tom pausing to adjust the black crêpe ribbons on both his and Duncan's hats, while Leah, head downcast just stood, gazing at nothing. The undertaker gave a signal that the procession was about to start, the mute took his place in front of the hearse, and gradually began the slow walk over the cobbles toward the base of the steps. Shopkeepers stood outside their premises, their heads bowed in respect, the Town Hall clock struck eleven. Stanhope reasoned to himself, if there was no family, at least there'd be nobody to argue with, or contest, the will, and his soon-to-be sister-in-law would have quite a handsome dowry.

Suddenly a seagull flying overhead splattered his hat.

Constance forced herself to suppress her mirth. It wasn't the right place or time—but she'd laugh about it later.

Weddings and funerals seemed so very far removed, but later that day Constance wrote (as was her usual weekly ritual) to Lynton to tell him her news. She had bought some table napkins for her bottom drawer, and had seen a dinner service with a green and gold rim which looked decidedly elegant and tasteful. Tureens, sauce boats with matching ladles, meat plates of various sizes, knife rests, and an afternoon tea service was available in the same pattern.

Papa seemed completely engrossed in his books. Ashley was keeping busy, but he and Leah had still not fixed a date for their wedding, though their house was now completely furnished and ready for occupation. Ashley had, however, intimated that he would, immediately the date for the wedding was set, write to him asking him to be his "man", and so be by his side on such an important occasion.

She was so—*so*—very much looking forward to their own wedding day, and sent all her love—all her very, *very* dear love.

Constance sighed and wiped away tears. She was beginning to ask herself if this wedding would ever happen. She looked in her mirror… and saw an old maid staring back.

Chapter 18

Morale was high, the air charged with expectation and anticipation and Lynton turned his face into the wind as he said farewell to England.

There was a crack of virgin canvas as the great ship moved, her sails open to heaven, rigging taut as tuned fiddle strings, leaving in the water a trail of spume pointing toward the land, and above the scream of the gulls, Lynton fancied he heard Constance calling him. Again the seabirds screamed as the man-o'-war glided belly deep over the emerald water. The land was becoming more distant: soon it would be a speck on the horizon, then there'd be nothing.

A ship of the line carried upwards of eight hundred men, a complete world in itself, it could stay at sea as long as the officers saw fit. Every three months, supply ships (or boats, if they were near port) would bring food and water, and if one was lucky, letters... and Lynton somehow *knew* that it would a long time before he saw land. He was not the best of sailors, and for days he could do no more than stagger to mess and watch his fellow officers eat, or he would rush to the side of the ship if he were unfortunate enough to see a greasy pool ooze from the salt pork on his plate.

In the noisy cockpit he heaved and rocked hourly in his hammock, the only consolation being that this nausea would eventually pass: time had taught him that lesson. Occasionally a yellow light from the cockpit hatch would penetrate the gloom, the swaying shadows being turned into grotesque shapes from the swinging lighted lanterns, and he would so very earnestly wish he could breathe his last. No longer did he hear, or at least, take any notice, of the ship's monotonous creaking, nor did he smell the stench of sickness and vomit, nor the close proximity of men's bodies, nor the sweating hulk of the ship.

He'd always been a poor sailor, but since his becoming ill—oh, how wonderful it would be to die!

But the feeling passed. Lynton Shaw was not going to be allowed to shake of his mortal coil, and as he struggled to reach the quarter-deck and the salt air, he shivered uncontrollably as he watched the tops of the masts swinging beneath the stars. The scanty contents of his stomach curdled and displayed themselves. One trembling hand went to his forehead, the other wiped the vomit from his chin and the front of his clothing.

A ship's surgeon who was seasick! It was ironic, but it could be worse, for he could be the ship's physician! Yet if it were any consolation he was not the only poor sailor on board. Several others were spewing their insides out, the ship, quite insensitive to their plight riding up and down—as they themselves had been but days before, as they serviced the harbourside whores. He fancied some of them had managed to stowaway—as indeed had some of the men's wives—but morals were the last thing on his mind.

As he miraculously found the strength to move about his floating world, he could tell that the previous sense of enthusiasm among the men had somewhat diminished. Earlier there'd been dancing to a lively hornpipe, and when a rating had made ribald jokes that there wasn't room in the bulkhead to "swing a cat"—the man had given a hollow laugh and removed his shirt to reveal the scars on his back of a past flogging.

Strange days. Men at sea revealed glimpses into their souls that landsmen would have kept hidden.

Lynton Shaw tried hard to keep his own secret, until he collapsed and was seen by the ship's physician, and his condition officially diagnosed.

Having had no communication from Lynton because (as Constance told herself) if he were at sea, as she supposed him to be, then she knew from experience that letters would be, at best, sporadic—and at worst, non-existent. Not knowing what was happening was the worst of it, and that was why she must be diligently reading the newspapers in order to keep herself up-to-date with the state of the war.

> *On the 18th. August Nelson's ship had arrived in Portsmouth, the following day he proceeded to London, and Merton south west of London, and three weeks later was in his carriage driving through Petersfield then Portsmouth Hill and across the waterway dividing Portsea Island from the mainland, finally arriving at the* George Hotel *in the High Street.*

September 14th, another edition told her that Nelson had:

> *…Arrived in Portsmouth and boarded the* Victory. *An enormous crowd had gathered and he strove to elude its attention by taking his boat at the bathing machines on Southsea Beach, instead of the usual landing place. However, a woman threw flowers at his feet, and men poured about him as if he were a Saint, eager to look at his face, sobbing and falling down before him in prayer.*

So well could she imagine the scene, and the patriotic fervour of the crowd, that she could close her eyes and see the charismatic figure, elegant in knee-breeches and satin stockings. Gracing his admiral's hat (although intended to be worn in a turban) she imagined he would be wearing the *chelengk* conferred upon him by Sultan Selim III of Turkey, to honour his victory at the Battle of the Nile. Studded with diamonds and the size of a hand, she had read somewhere that it contained a tiny clockwork device that moved the jewels around.

Yes, he would definitely—defiantly—be wearing such a decoration!

Two days later Constance read in The Times-
> *It is a circumstance not unworthy of remark in connection with the success which has invariably attended Lord Nelson that the wind which has blown to the Westward and to other points which was foul for sailing for a considerable time past shifted on Saturday a few minutes after his Lordship reached the Victory. At eight o' clock yesterday morning the Victory got underway and by twelve she had cleared the Isle of Man.*

On the same day she also read:
> *The gallant Vice-Admiral Sir T. Duckworth K.B. has received his appointment as Second in Command to the brave Vice Admiral Lord Nelson. It is supposed he will hoist his flag on board the Ajax of 74 guns now in Cawsand Bay ready to join him with the Thunderer of 74 guns on his appearance to the S.E. of the Eddystone.*

The following morning there was further information in The Times:
> *Arrived this morning at eight o' clock The Victory of 100 guns. Vice Admiral Lord Nelson in company with a frigate which he sent in to call of the ships ready here when the Ajax and Thunderer of 74 guns apiece each sailed to join them.*

The September 29th paper said:
> *Nelson joined the fleet off Cadiz. "The reception I met with on joining the fleet," Nelson wrote to a friend, "caused the sweetest sensation of my life."*

And Constance could imagine the feeling among the men—and she was so very proud that her Lynton was to be part of it.

October 8th. Constance read that:
> *Nelson had an inshore squadron of five frigates and two schooners off Cadiz, and had stationed three fast-sailing 74 gun ships Mars, Defiance and Colossus nine to twelve miles between the fleet and Cadiz "in order that I may get information from the frigates as expeditiously as possible."*

The October 15th edition read:

> In the previous two weeks there had been an almost continuous movement of ships, and by October 15th. the British fleet had reached its full strength of 27 ships of the line and 5 frigates, as the force which would meet the combined fleet a week later.

Although there had been no letters from Lynton regarding these things, Constance knew—she just *knew*—that he would be part of this convoy, and so very, very proud she felt as she walked through Whitby, her head held high.

Why—she thought—he might even be the surgeon on board the *Victory!* That really would be something to boast about.

Chapter 19

Leah's time for grieving had to come to an end, for she and Ashley had finally "named the day": the first Saturday in November.

It was to be a morning wedding, at eleven-thirty, and, being only weeks away, there was much to be done in a short space of time. There was the wedding breakfast to organise, dresses to get made, thank-you letters to write, as presents started to arrive, staff to engage to ensure the smooth running of the Langden's new home, Elijah to move to his new quarters… and Ashley? Well, he'd have things to see-to as well.

Leah went through the house that had for so many years been her home, collecting this-and-that and packing box after box with her personal effects. More than once had she looked longingly at the silver candlesticks and the silver cupids pulling chariots, reminders of their exodus from the plague-stricken hamlet where they'd been born. She would handle them, and be tempted—then return them to their cupboard. She must talk to Tom about them, when the moment presented itself.

And if Tom and Sarah… then what would become of Duncan?

The matter of settling his future had only just occurred to her. She and Tom couldn't just abandon him, yet somehow she didn't see him fitting into her new life with Ashley. And if Tom and Sarah were to set up home together, then would they be prepared have him live with them? Not that he was any trouble, and he was a big help to Tom…

Then another thought occurred to her. Sarah was a wealthy woman: perhaps Tom wouldn't need to work ever again, and the apothecary's would be sold. What then would become of Duncan?

Yet there was always the chance that…

Her anxious thoughts were interrupted by a voice calling, "Leah, it's me!"—and seconds later Constance appeared. Shaking her cloak before removing it, she said simply, "I do hope Ashley's having fires regularly burning in your new home. The afternoons are getting chilly. And there's a mean wind blowing off the sea today."

"Mmm."

"And has he had words with Tom yet?"—and seeing the vacant look on her friend's face answered her own question. "No, I can see he hasn't. I'll remind him. *Men!*"

"He's very busy 'workwise'." Leah made excuses for him.

"So I understand. That Mrs Dalgleish woman is *forever* singing his praises."

"Oh, her. She came into the shop yesterday and, being the worse for drink, she came out with a mouthful of the most unladylike language."

"But she does it so politely, doesn't she."

"Yes," Leah had to agree, then added, "I suppose it's to do with her *profession*—if one can call it that."

"Being a brothel keeper, do you mean?"

"And quite open about it—she really has no shame."

"None at all. But on a different topic: is there anything to do with your wedding plans that I can help with? I know mine seems miles away—and might never happen. Therefore I must keep busy—and keep hoping!"

"It really is an important job I'm asking you to take on, and I shall quite understand if you feel you must decline"—and Ashley Langden looked at his lifelong friend Tom Metcalfe before continuing, "being my man at my wedding—well, it involves such a lot of responsibilities. You have to make sure the wedding ring is in your waistcoat pocket, you'll have to make speeches, kiss all my aunts and things like this… and that's why… I think you'll need the help of this young man as well," and he turned to Duncan and gave a sigh. "It all depends on you now. Can you keep your big brother in order, and make sure he doesn't do anything silly on the day?"

"Is he going to be the only one to kiss all the young girls?" Tom pulled a face, "and dance with them, and whisper things? It isn't fair."

"Well, it's that or nothing. Duncan here will have to make sure you behave yourself. Now Duncan, what do you say? Are you going to be my man as well? It will make Leah very happy if you say yes."

"Yes," Duncan replied without hesitation.

"And you'll have identical posh suits, with top hats and smart shoes. We must get you both to the tailors as soon as possible, for there's much to do, and so little time to do it in—and I must be away. I've things to get ready for tomorrow morning."

"I'll let you out—that shop door's difficult." And as Tom followed him down the stairs and the two were out of earshot, he slapped his friend on the back. "Thanks, Ash. About Duncan, I mean. The lad's really pleased."

"You'd best let Leah know."

"You mean—?"

"Duncan? Oh no, that was my idea. She knows nothing about it"—and he stepped into the autumn night air and hurried along Church Street towards home. His father and Constance would no doubt be in the library: they were very bookish persons, and might never have realised that he'd been out. Now he had done the deed, he felt he had betrayed his friend Lynton. But, he reasoned, it could be years before Lynton Shaw set foot on dry land again—if he ever did!

"But who is going to give me away?"

Tom paused aghast as he was bringing the mug of tea to his lips.

"I'm sorry, Leah. He just asked us and we said yes without thinking. Although we've grown up together, I thought he'd ask one of his brothers. I just wasn't prepared... shall I tell him I've had time to think and—"

"And spoil Duncan's day? No—definitely no. We'll... oh—I don't know. I don't suppose it has to be a man... I know it's usually the bride's father or some other close relative who gives her away—but it could be a woman."

"Anyone in mind?" he asked hopefully.

"Yes. Hannah."

Seeing the look on his face, Leah quickly went on to explain, "After all, she was helping uncle Nathan when we first arrived on his doorstep. She's been like a second mum to me. Now Sarah's only a few years older than I am—so I couldn't think of asking *her*, could I?"

"No. Not really..."

"Then that's settled. I'll ask Hannah first thing in the morning."

Weddings—weddings—weddings! It was Leah's only topic of conversation.

Nor was there any getting away from the subject even in the shop, for customers were constantly calling with presents and gossip, or old women would presume to offer "advice" for the bride-to-be on her wedding night—certainly not for the ears of menfolk—and it seemed the only escape for Tom and Duncan was at Sarah's.

"I shall be so pleased when this 'wedding of the year'—as Leah and Constance refer to it—is over. Just two more weeks to the big day."

"And after that?"

"Well," and Tom ruffled Duncan's hair, "this young man will have to do all the cooking and cleaning, and he'll be up at five o' clock riddling out the grate before lighting the fire, then he'll bring me my breakfast in bed and put out my clothes for the day... and he'll have all the washing to do—and shopping, and..."

"Don't take any notice, Duncan, he's just teasing." Then, suddenly serious, Sarah asked, "will you be all right—I mean, I could always—"

"No, we'll be fine," Tom assured her, "and Leah has to lead her own life, for after all, she's been planning to marry Ashley ever since we were children… and they've been betrothed for over twelve months. We all knew it would happen, sooner or later."

"And it's a very big house, where they're going to live, and they'll be taking Elijah with them!"—and Duncan pulled a face, adding, "I wish *we* could have a parrot."

"We've got two cats."

"—Not the same as a parrot."

"I'll dress you up in feathers and keep you in a cage. How'd you like that?"

"Better still, let's dress Tom up in feathers—what d'you say to that, Duncan?"

"Yes," Duncan agreed, "and poke him with a stick—and make him say 'who's a pretty boy'?"

"Oh! Tom Metcalfe"—and Sarah pretended to be very concerned, "I can see you'll have no peace. Duncan's going to take you in-hand… so… you'd better take a few minutes rest while you can, and Duncan and I will make some supper."

Then she added, "I do hope you're hungry. I've cooked a salmon."

"Lovely!"

"Come on, Duncan."

Sarah paused from her chores, watching her helper carefully arrange the cutlery. He gave a quizzical glance at his handiwork, then slightly moved a fork, before asking, "Is that all right?"

"And we'll need some fruit spoons. We're having a pudding for afters."

"I like your puddings."

"This one's made with apples from Lady Celia's garden, Duncan—and there's some cream from Far Clough…"—and taking advantage of them being on their own, Sarah voiced a subject that she'd been secretly mulling over for days. "I don't know—well… I suppose Tom has mentioned… what might happen to the three of us after Leah gets married to Ashley?"

"…You *could* come to live with us."

"That's possible. And if we do live together… well, I could be, let's say, like a 'sister' to you, as Leah is, or I could be… an aunt… or… "

"Yes?"

Sarah took a deep breath. "Or I could be your mum."

The boy stood motionless. After what seemed an eternity, Sarah finally asked, "well, what do you say?"

"You can have lots of aunts," he reasoned, "and lots of elder sisters... but you can only have one mum. Sarah... I'd like you to be my mum."

She held back her tears as she hugged him close.

There was great commotion about the quayside, lots of shouting and men staring out to sea, where even greater arguments were raging. For the Admiralty had now ordered officers commanding warships together with press-gangs to ignore the until-then protected status of whalers, and the ship *Orlando,* within sight of the harbour, had been intercepted and all her crew impressed, save for two men who jumped overboard and struck out in the direction of the cliffs beneath the abbey. Guns were fired, and it was not known if the men were alive or dead.

Later that evening there were brawls in the inns, which spilled out into the streets and yards—Whitby was suddenly a dangerous place to be.

Constance received the communication only two days before her brother and Leah's wedding, and as she read, and re-read the contents, the emotion welling up inside her. Close to tears, she handed the Admiralty document to her father.

He read it in silence, then asked, "What are you going to do?"

"Well... I must go to London. I need to be at his side—but there's... Papa, we must keep this to ourselves, for now, anyway. When the wedding's over, first thing Monday morning I'll get the London coach. Could you make the arrangements today? I shall need to get some money from the bank. I'll do that now—and we... we must *tell no-one*. I don't want *anything* to spoil Ashley and Leah's big day."

Her father understood, and agreed to comply with her wishes.

The morning of the wedding dawned, and Tom and Duncan were roused by their soon-to-be brother-in-law, who, it seemed had been up and about for hours. The three of them breakfasted, leaving what they now called "Leah's kitchen" spotlessly clean and tidy, tossed a coin for who should have the first bath and while Duncan immersed himself in hot soapy suds the two men went about their ablutions, stropped cut-throat razors then scraped away clouds of lather and stubble underneath. Duncan jumped out of the bath tub and Tom jumped in, Ashley boiled more water, then when it was his turn self-consciously stared at his anatomy and thought about... when the wedding ceremony was over... and... later that night when he and Leah would be on their own, and they'd retire to the four-poster bed with pale blue drapes—and, he imagined, they'd do... *that*.

What if nothing stirred down there?

Or supposing Leah didn't know what was supposed to happen on their wedding night—what then?

It was all right the bride being innocent and inexperienced—but for the husband? He should be the one with...

He suddenly felt ashamed that he'd never—that he was still a virgin.

"Tom... er... you've nothing at the shop in one of those drawers that... you know... tonight..."

Tom and Duncan kept straight faces. *"Ye-es...?"*

"Come on, you know what I'm getting at."

"Even *I* know," Duncan grinned.

"Anyway," Tom reasoned, "it's bad luck to see your bride until the actual ceremony, which is why we've stayed here with you. We daren't call in the shop this morning, it'll be chaotic."

"I know, but..."

"Besides, what's in those drawers in the back room are for old men. And I don't suppose it works anyway. Don't worry. It's meant to be the bride needs advice, not the feller. Now, come on, Duncan—let's see you all dolled-up in your finery, and we'll leave Ashley to wash his bits and pieces..." Tom's eyes travelled down Ashley Langden's body and a smile creased his cheeks.

Constance put on a brave face, for she was determined that nothing should spoil the day.

Leah, in the dress with forget-me-nots, over which was to be worn a looped train trimmed with blue lace, had on her feet satin bottines, and to complete the ensemble she would wear long lace gloves and a bonnet with feathers.

Hannah, in dark blue velvet brocade, fussed like a mother hen while the bridesmaid, plumes in her hair, rouge on her cheeks and a large ring worn over her gloves, tried yet again to concentrate on the business in hand, and not let her dark thoughts wander. She went to the window and looked out onto a cold grey morning. Elijah gave a non-committal squawk.

The clock struck the hour. It was ten o' clock. Minutes were as years--nd Constance yet again mentally planned the journey she must soon make, and felt more than a twinge of envy at the thought of the happiness that would soon be Leah's. Her thoughts again began to roam...

The cake! Fruit cake to ensure a fruitful marriage, the bride needing to keep a portion of the wedding cake to ensure a loving and faithful husband. There was also the groom's cake, placed beside the bride's cake, but to be cut up and boxed for the wedding guests to take home. A girl who slept with a slice of groom's cake under her pillow would dream of her future husband—and she suddenly remembered that the bride must wear no make-up during the ceremony, nor have her face covered, or the marriage would not be legal and binding.

For make-up was considered an "ensnarement"—a marriage trap!

If only...!

The three men, in immaculate identical morning suits, two of them boisterous, one slightly nervous, sat in silence in the front right-hand pew of St Mary's.

"'Cold," Ashley murmured.

"Bloody cold," Tom agreed as he looked around him—at an altar decorated with flowers, as were the ends of each pew. There were also big bunches of white chrysanthemums and trailing greenery in the porch, and the florist had done floral arrangements for the windows. The organist commenced with somewhat indifferent sounds before suddenly bellowing forth with a strident voluntary, as the first guests were being ushered into their places. The music died down as suddenly as it had crashed about their ears, and was now nothing more than an dusty asthmatic wheeze.

Ashley broke silence. "You could be next."

"Eh?"

"You and Sarah."

"Oh... well, you never know"—and Duncan, hearing this, gave Tom a playful nudge. The lad felt "restrained" in his clothes: he would have felt much happier if indeed it had been Tom and Sarah who were getting married. He stared round the interior of St Mary's, at the wooden roof, with its numerous skylights. It would, he imagined, be not unlike below-decks of a ship of the line. Then his gaze came to rest on the long high gallery along the south wall of the nave, and from there travelled to the galleries at the west end and to the church walls hung with wooden tablets on which were painted religious texts; obscuring the beauty of the chancel and the delicacy of the chancel arch, the Cholmley pew.

Above them hung a great candelabra, its florid lines suggesting an Italian origin. This, Tom had earlier told him, was lit for the torchlight burial services of the well-to-do of Whitby, nor was it supposed to be lit at any other time. Folk were even, according to Tom, buried under the church, and beneath the large blue stone in the chancel floor was laid Sir Richard Cholmley, and on the mural monument to his memory were three hands, symbolising the three great families from which he claimed descent. On each thumb was a ring, and on both of these were three little ringlets, symbolising the Trinity.

But, as Tom had also assured him, the Cholmleys were a family far removed from most.

The organist again struck up, and Tom turned to look. Then he reported to Ashley, "thee uncle Edgar and aunt Isobel."

"Is Cedric with them?"

"Spotty lad, with a gormless look?"

Ashley nodded.

"Yes, he's arrived as well."

The organist struck a thunderous chord fit to rouse the dead, followed by a long cadenza as more of Ashley's relatives were led to their pews, and Tom (it was now his turn to stare) fixed his gaze on the three-tiered pulpit supported on iron props attached to the right and left hand pews of the middle aisle, forming an arch by which to approach the chancel steps. The organ was again playing with a muffled woolly sound as he looked toward the communion table with its red cover and red tasselling at each corner, to the altar, the stained glass windows depicting saints and displaying coats-of-arms...

More guests arrived. Westwood and Beatrice and their offspring, who were making themselves comfortable in the pew behind them. Beatrice wore drab brown, complemented by a shiny red face eyes looking in different directions. Wearing glowing vestments, the vicar, all smiles, was coming down the aisle toward them. The church now boasted numerous people in various pews, though the left side of the church looked sparse, with only a group of Leah's friends, who were whispering and giggling.

"What's the time?" and the groom tried to rush out to relieve himself behind one of the headstones, but was restrained from doing so by Tom, who announced, "Only a few more minutes—and far too late to change your mind."

"I wasn't going to do that, but... a call of nature, you know."

Tom shook his head. "It mun save."

Suddenly inside the porch there was a flurry of activity. Someone gave the signal and the organist burst into Handel's *Lascia Ch'io Pianga* from his opera *Rinaldo* as the bride, on Hannah's arm and with Constance following close behind, slowly made her way down the aisle. The groom and his men stood to attention, as the wedding ceremony between Leah Metcalfe and Ashley Langden was solemnised.

After the marriage register had been signed and witnessed, the bells of St Mary's rang out, and as the newly-married couple walked down the aisle, well-wishers offered their congratulations. Beneath the Royal Coat-of-Arms under the staircase leading to the south gallery there was the customary kiss, under the aegis of the French *fleur-de-lys* and the Horse of Hanover rampant. As the peal of six bells rang out, young men, regardless of the flurry of snow, raced down the Donkey Steps to see who should be the first at the bride's new house, thus winning the privilege of removing the bridal garter from Leah's leg.

In-laws shook hands, Duncan evidently enjoying himself and showing off all the French phrases he'd learned. There was Tom hovering, and the happy couple kissing aunts and uncles and looking blissfully happy.

Suddenly Leah turned to Tom. "I was wondering… could you place my flowers on uncle Nathan's grave?"

"Why yes—that's a lovely gesture"—and Tom searched for Sarah who, although an invited guest, must nevertheless have been feeling somewhat neglected. She would welcome the duty.

The two of them stepped outside past waiting carriages, their horses, never better turned-out, neighing and spluttering as the snowflakes fell like confetti.

"Here he is." Tom stopped at the foot of the mound of broken earth. "There's not been time to arrange anything with the stonemason yet, being so busy with the—"

He stopped abruptly as Sarah grabbed his arm.

She pointed to a figure darting between the headstones. She was shaking all over as eventually she blurted out, "That man we saw running away—it's Cain!"

The wedding breakfast that followed was no more than a vague dream to Sarah as the various dishes passed in front of her. Lobster salad; collared eel; fowls in *Béchamel* sauce; ribs of lamb; mayonnaise of salmon; raised pies, both ham and pigeon; garnished tongues; larded capons; roast chicken; veal-and-ham pie; trout; sauces and jellies; various breads and accompaniments—all went unnoticed, some even untouched.

Similarly the *charlotte rousse a-la vanilla;* blancmanges; fruit tarts; Devonshire junket; syllabubs; *compôtes* of fruits; angels' hair cream; *crème brulée;* cakes and pastries and other things for the wedding guests—for her appetite had disappeared on seeing *him.*

Despite his unkempt appearance, plus the beard he now wore (rarely though was he was ever clean, certainly never smartly-dressed), it was unmistakeably *him*. Now she knew the truth: not only was Cain Dacre still alive—he was in Whitby.

Chapter 20

The morning was crisp, the cobbles white and glistening, as Constance boarded the London-bound coach. Outwardly brave for the benefit of her father, who was helping to organise her luggage, deep inside she was indeed fearful as to what lay in store for her.

"Give Lynton our best wishes for a speedy recovery, and"—he paused to take an envelope from his pocket—"a little something extra. London could be more expensive than you think. And if, for any reason you find yourself short of money… still, you'll only be away a few days."

"Yes, papa, and thank you." Travellers were already making themselves comfortable for the long journey. The coachman was seated up in his box. Constance hated travelling in general, and this trip to London in particular. But it was a journey she had to make.

Sarah also was filled with trepidation as she and Tom entered the chambers of Stanhope Langden and began to tell their tale. Their advocate listened, and after the inevitable advice that they should be extra-vigilant, the couple left for the apothecary's shop. They had decided Sarah would be safer there than if she were on her own. Alone with his thoughts, Stanhope pondered on the supposition, indeed the wild, fanciful notion… that one of the men who jumped overboard when the impress-men boarded the whaler might possibly have been none other than Cain Dacre. Two men had escaped, but only one body had been washed ashore.

He tried to dismiss the idea. It was against all odds… but it was nevertheless feasible.

Having exchanged pleasantries with her travelling companions Constance stared out of the coach window to view a raw morning and an overcast sky, and had to admit (albeit somewhat reluctantly, and then, only to herself) that, because of the correspondence she had earlier received, things were not as she had for weeks past pictured them to be. Lynton had not been horribly war-wounded, or suffered even the slightest injuries. He would not be able to proudly sport battle scars—because he had not been in any battle. Her fantasies that he was on board the *Victory* assisting the main surgeon had been just that—fantasies!

But nevertheless, hearing that he had been invalided out of the Navy and had been ill for many weeks, and had only recently been transferred to Greenwich Hospital where he was being cared for, was just as disturbing. She closed her eyes and imagined what the place might be like, and what she would find on her arrival, and she pulled her cloak over her shoulders, becoming more and more engrossed in her thoughts—oblivious of the changing landscape, oblivious of anything and everything.

"A certain Mr O'Connor is outside, Sir." Stanhope's clerk gave a respectful cough.

"Give me a couple of minutes, then send him in." Stanhope continued reading, then signing the letters on his desk until his clerk reappeared, said simply, "Mr O'Connor, Sir," and discreetly withdrew.

"Now then, what's the latest harbourside gossip?"

"Nothing to report, Sir."

"Well, I have. Regarding a certain Cain Dacre. Would it surprise you to learn that he's in Whitby—or at least was seen in Whitby only days ago?"

The Irishman stared as the lawyer continued, "There's no doubt about it. Now—you need to be on your guard. He could simply sign-on with the next ship leaving Whitby... or hang about the harbour, making friends with the other quayside scum. And one of them might possibly mention... that you have certain information for him, in which case he will, as you had planned, come looking for you."

Malahide swallowed nervously. "You think he might do that, Mr Langden?"

"Well, that's what you wanted, isn't it?"

"And if he does?"

"Then agree to meet him—but let me know in advance, and I can arrange for his apprehension, leading to his trial. If this works in our favour, then you'll be well-rewarded."

"And if it doesn't?"

Stanhope Langden looked heavenward—words were quite unnecessary—and the Irishman took his leave.

Later that day Stanhope and his clerk visited the harbour where the whaler *Orlando* was at anchor. Only the captain had been allowed to remain with her, and she now seemed like a doomed ship—for no man would be fool enough to sign-on for a voyage that could end as her previous one had. The clerk made enquiries, and Stanhope was allowed to see the ship's log and the names of the crew. It was as he had supposed. He saw the name, and alongside it, the man's signature.

"And they were all impressed?"

"Except for"—and the captain pointed out two names. "They jumped overboard. One of them drowned."

Stanhope thanked him. His next port-of-call was the church at Hinderwell, near Staithes, where he asked to examine the marriage register to compare signatures.

It was a place that filled her with dread, even before she saw it and, caring to do little but speculate on what she might find on her arrival, Constance put off her visit till the very last moment. She tried to convince herself that within days, a week at the very most, the two of them would be on their way back to Whitby, where she would take it upon herself to nurse him back to health. Surely the bracing sea air, and walks along the cliffs, would speed his recovery a thousand times more than being in a ward with lots of ailing men.

Tom and Ashley would advise on medications. They would even help her, should she need to call on them, and then… when he was fit and well, a few weeks hence, say, they could fix a date for their wedding and live happily ever after.

Marriage couldn't come soon enough!

Chapter 21

Lynton Shaw shuffled and drew his sheets closer as his companion in the next bed, a now-blind naval rating, related yet again his tale. A story that was beginning to lose its lustre, were it not for the elaborations and embellishments that managed (sometimes) to give a new twist to its telling.

"It was a lovely calm morning, with a breeze so light it scarcely ruffled the sea, when the French and Spanish fleet were sighted. There were seventeen thousand of us staring toward the far horizon, counting thirty three enemy ships in a column five miles long—and we sighted them before they saw us, for the light was behind them. But of course," the narrator continued, and Lynton drifted into a half-sleep, only to be roused with the cry "'Prepare for Battle'—and at seven o' clock the squadron had begun to draw up in a line. Two hours later the enemy ships were five miles distant."

Lynton tried to control his coughing bout. Yet again he felt deeply ashamed that he should have been declared unfit for service when, by rights, he should have been part of this scenario, and he could well imagine the fervour, the excitement onboard the men-o'-war. He could visualise the men stripped to the waist, barefooted, kerchiefs round their heads to help deaden the noise of the guns, and imagine the dapper officers, elegant in frock coats with epaulettes, immaculate knee-breeches, silk stockings and shoes with silver buckles as opposed to boots, so as to make it more manageable for the surgeon should they be shot in the leg. A complete contrast between two worlds: the mere "men"—and their masters.

"…And they were making their wills, verbally, of course. One would say to his friend "if I die, then I leave everything to you, but if you get killed and I survive, do you promise the same?—Then shake on 't, and let's get 'parson to witness."

Lynton visualised the partitions, which until then had formed the officers' cabins around the aft guns, being dismantled, the nettings above the bulwarks covered in hammocks to offer some sort of protection for those on the exposed upper decks, while on the lowest deck, the area most protected from the inevitable gunfire that would ensue becoming the domain of the ship's surgeon. The medicine chests and bandages would be in position, sails prepared for the wounded to be placed on.

Every available bucket and tub would be filled with water to douse the inevitable fires, superfluous ship's stores would be thrown overboard:

bags of flour, casks of beef... Lynton could picture the scene, see the wooden barrels bobbing about among the discarded items.

He could even imagine the men at the guns enjoying a meal of bread and cheese washed down with beer; the forced bravado before battle, waving cutlasses, even dancing hornpipes, the tension being relieved by music. For "bands" seemed to convene themselves of any volunteers among the crew, who would improvise and use barrels for drums, bent ramrods for triangles, and whatever in the way of bassoons or oboes had been looted from captured enemy ships. They would all be playing different tunes, some very badly, the overall effect a cheerful one.

A far cry from the *Rogues' March* beaten on drums before a flogging!

He could picture the ship's surgeons testing the edges of their knives and scalpels and the bite of their amputating saws. Making sure that their forceps for removing gunshot were on-hand, tourniquets, bandages and dressings. He could hear men screaming; see their guts spilling on the decks as they were carried to the cockpit below, the forever slimy gangways made even more treacherous with blood and sprays of green spume as enemy shot hit the water. The violent rocking of the ship, the shrieks of the wounded drowned by the roar and pounding of the cannons overhead, as the trucks bearing them strained and crashed against the restraining ropes.

He could hear more thundering from the guns, and see billowing clouds of smoke as loblolly boys brought the wounded down to the cockpit; the dying to be thrown overboard, bright bloodstained bodies contrasting sharply with the intense green of the sea, a final trail of blood spurting from each body and streaking the surface like the veins running through Carrera marble.

He could see all this—even though he had not been part of it.

As Constance stood and stared in wonder at the magnificent building which now served as the Seaman's Hospital at Greenwich, her earlier fears (albeit temporarily) vanished. She thought only of its history and the royal associations of the Greenwich Palace, as was. The birthplace of Henry the Eighth; and when he grew up the scene of much entertaining and feasting. It had been here that the Monarch had married Catherine of Aragon; where their daughter, Mary Tudor, had been born; here also that he wed Anne of Cleves, and where Anne Boleyn gave birth to their daughter Elizabeth.

Constance was drawn back into the past and found herself a part of Queen Elizabeth's summer court, the Palace being the scene of a spectacular water pageant, pipes and drums competing with the celebratory guns and fireworks. The river was crowded with all manner of craft, from the brilliantly painted royal barge to simple rowing boats. She saw the Queen in all her jewelled finery, her red hair dressed and adorned with pearls, fingers heavy with jewels. As the entourage approached the Palace she heard a sudden fanfare of trumpets, then witnessed the ultimate in gallantry as a courtier cast his cloak on the ground for the Queen to walk on as she stepped from the barge.

As Constance experienced this moment in history—re-living it—a sudden cold gust from the river made her shudder as though someone were stepping on her grave. In those few moments when her mind was wandering, had she somehow disturbed some spirit of the past—a royal princess or prince? Who could tell?

But the moment was gone, never to return.

As she made her way toward the entrance of the hospital, she ceased her rambling thoughts and concentrated on the more immediate, and to her, more personal problems. Not for the first time that day, niggling thoughts began to tug at her. Supposing Lynton really were ill—or his condition had deteriorated? What would she do if—?

But she banished such discouraging thoughts. Everything would be fine.

In the hallway footsteps echoed on the mosaic floor. She stopped. No, it was not as she'd earlier imagined, but the footsteps of a young woman in a simple grey dress, over which was a threadbare cloak. Constance turned: the stranger gave a nervous smile, and seeming quite bewildered began, "If you please, mum... "

"Yes?"

"My husband's had his leg shot off, and I've come to visit, only... I don't know where to go... who to ask for directions or anything. It's the first time I've been, you see, and..." her voice tailed off, and Constance read the fear in her eyes. Fear of what she might see.

"Then we shall make our enquiries together," Constance spoke kindly to the distressed woman, "for I feel exactly as you do, as this is my first visit too."

Biting her knuckles, the woman continued, "My Thomas was press-ganged into service. What about your man—or am I being presumptuous? Perhaps you're here to visit your brother, or—"

"I'm visiting my fiancé—and we're soon to be married."

"My man's called Alistair," the woman repeated. "What's yours called?"

"Lynton. Lynton Shaw. He was a surgeon, till he was taken ill. Now he's... very weak. But we have to be brave, just as our men were"—and Constance grew quite resolute. "They are fearless, courageous heroes who have served their King and Country, and when we come face-to-face with them, we too must be brave, and give them all our comfort and love. Let us find some physician—someone in authority—who can show us to their wards, advise us on their condition."

"I'm... a bit scared of seeing Alistair for the first time since his... 'leg' business... and..."

"Then I shall come with you"—and Constance, who had already won the young woman's confidence, took command of the situation.

Minutes later an orderly was directing the two women to a ward full of injured men, where Constance came face to face with, and learned the true meaning of the word *suffering*. Their nostrils were assailed with the awful sweet stench of open sores and rotting gangrene. All around them were discarded bloodstained dressings, the men displaying wounds, pus-encrusted from earlier burn-marks of cauterizing irons, and angry flesh, shiny red and tight with infection. There were men blinded by the flash of gunpowder, a young man shot in the spine and now paralysed, another with a ball still embedded in his thigh, a dirty rag tied round his hip while his companion was airing a stump below his knee which looked like raw liver. Men unashamedly exhibited open wounds, some seeping, other scabbing over, a man with both his legs shot off...

Then her companion gave a sudden scream and turned to run—from a man with a stump for a leg and half his face missing.

Constance gripped her hand, and the two of them looked hard at the woman's husband. There were tears in his eyes as his wife whispered, "My poor Alistair, my poor love."

He tried to speak, but made sounds little better than an animal. And as Constance looked around her at the hideously maimed and wounded, she wondered if it would not have been better, certainly kinder, if the battle had claimed their lives as well. For these fearless men would carry the marks of Trafalgar to their graves: their hacked-off limbs, their sightless eyes, their once-handsome faces now mutilated for ever—these were the real war medals!

To Constance Langden there was no longer anything fine or noble about this war. Nothing at all.

Lynton was looking pale, and, as she expected him to be, "tired".

But he was alive, that was the main thing. Explanations and the like would come later. She took his hand and whispered, "I'm... so pleased to see you." And she looked again, and saw the young God with the fiery copper mane that had first travelled to Whitby with Ashley. A robust, healthy young man, full of life and forever laughing. Sadly, all that had now left Lynton Shaw.

She stared at him in disbelief. His hair was long and dishevelled, cheeks were sunken, his bony fingers icy cold. There was a new subservience in his manner, and in an almost frightened voice he asked, "What are you thinking?"

"That you need lots of loving care to nurse you back to health"—she put on a brave face—"and until you feel well enough to travel to Whitby... then I shall take rooms for us in London—and care for you myself. I have a special syrup here that Tom has made up for you—and Ashley and Leah send their love, and hope to see you soon."

"How is Ashley?"

"Oh—surviving. You know my brother. Only recently married: I would imagine he and Leah are still on honeymoon. And—who can tell?—I could be an aunt this time next year."

He smiled. "Oh that's good news. You must offer my congratulations."

"You'll be able to do that yourself in a few weeks time"—and Constance held back her tears, for she knew in her heart that their time together would be short-lived. Every day had to be special: not a moment to be wasted.

Chapter 22

Two days after her arrival in London came news of the death of the much-loved Admiral. On 6th November there was an article in The Times which read:

We do not know whether we should mourn or rejoice. The country has gained the most splendid and decisive victory that has ever graced the annals of England: but it has been dearly purchased. The great and gallant Nelson is no more.

The following day the dispatch was published in full, together with Collingwood's expression of his great sorrow:

My heart is rent with the most poignant grief for the loss of a friend—a grief to which even the glorious occasion in which he fell does not bring the consolation which perhaps it ought.

On hearing of Nelson's death the Poet Laureate, Robert Southey, wrote: *men started at the intelligence and turned pale as if they had of the death of a dear friend*—and although it was the usual practice to bury at sea all those killed in battle, Hardy and the *Victory* officers knew England would wish to honour his remains, hence the preserving of him in a barrel of brandy. Plans were immediately made for a state funeral. It would certainly be in London, Constance reasoned, and might even take place before she and Lynton headed back to Yorkshire.

She'd be glad to get him away from the Greenwich Hospital, which seemed to her nothing more than a ship on dry land, with its accommodation in four "courts", or quarters of the hospital—each with naval names—and each ward being partitioned into cabins for single occupants or small groups. There were upwards of two-and-a-half thousand in-pensioners, each wearing a number showing where in the hospital they belonged, making it seem more like a prison than a charitable institution, with a strictly-ordered regime even for food.

The rations were 1lb of meat, boiled or roasted, beef three days, mutton two, and on Wednesdays and Fridays pease pottage, 8oz of cheese and 2oz butter. There was also a daily allowance of 4oz cheese, 1lb bread and a half gallon of beer, cabbage being the only green vegetable, but available throughout the year. The hospital had its own bakery and brewery, the entire military department being overseen by a governor, a lieutenant-governor, four hospital captains, eight lieutenants and two chaplains.

Senior Pensioners were appointed as under-lieutenants, and boatswains, one to each ward, with two mates as assistants. These men wore braided uniforms and their duties included ensuring that all pensioners shaved regularly, plus looking after their clothes and hospital property. It was also their duty to see all (except the sick) attended daily chapel—or they could be fined, being in breach of their duty, or in extreme cases, expelled. Any disciplines that were meted out were in keeping with naval traditions (though flogging was excluded) and fines, penalties and loss of liberties were enforced to maintain good conduct.

There were also "out-pensions" paid, of £7 a year for naval casualties being supported in the community. But Constance had already decided how Lynton would be supported—by herself!

The new Mr and Mrs Langden, looking radiant after their honeymoon, returned to a Whitby rousing itself for yet another festive season.

Shops were displaying their Christmas delights. The jet shop that had opened earlier in the year—the first of its kind in the town—displayed stock pins set in silver, also rings and necklaces carved from the peculiar fossilised wood found locally in the cliffs, laid down over a hundred-and-eighty million years ago. Tea dealers had boxed teas; spirit merchants had "special reserve" cognac—inviting one to believe it had been imported legally before the War—sweet shops had boxes of crystallised fruits; boot and shoe makers had their windows full of sensible winter footwear; milliners and dressmakers had mannequins displaying the latest fashion; butchers were taking orders for Christmas geese or turkeys to grace the Christmas table, stand pies, game or pork according to the customer's preference; while the bakery on Skinner Street had a window full of fruit cakes, and that renowned Whitby speciality: gingerbread covered in gold leaf.

Ashley seemed somewhat concerned on hearing about his friend Lynton, though his father was unable to say with any certainty the extent of his condition, other than that Constance had felt that she should be at his side, hence her hasty departure two days after the wedding.

"Well, if she's still in London over the Christmas period, then you must come to us on Christmas Day," Leah offered to Mr Langden senior.

"Why, that's very kind of you, Leah."

"And when you write to Constance, send her all our love"—and Leah felt so sorry for the old man as she and Ashley took their leave to call on Tom and Duncan.

"Apart from Constance being in London, have we missed anything?"—and Leah looked about her at the so-familiar surroundings that were no longer hers, now she was mistress of the house in Bagdale.

"The vassell singers have been—oh, and there's been hell-to-pay with the new Preventative Officer. It seems he was given the wrong tip-off, and whilst he and his men were lying in-wait higher up the coast, enough gin and brandy to float a battleship was smuggled ashore. It's 'somewhere along Baxtergate'—in one of the hidden cellars used for such contraband."

"And Sarah's made some Christmas puddings: she even let me help her." Duncan opened a cupboard and proudly displayed a sample of his own handiwork.

"Is Sarah... not here?"

"Out shopping"—Tom gave a discreet cough—"but she's staying here with me and Duncan for the time being"—and he tried to make light of the new situation.

"Well... you two men have somebody to care for you after all!"

Tom grinned. "You could say that."

News came that after repairs in Gibraltar the *Victory*, in the company of the *Belleisle*, would sail for England.

When she arrived on the 4th. December, plans for the funeral of the naval hero were well underway. The Prince of Wales, so the papers said, had planned to attend in his official capacity, but the King had forbidden it. Nor were there, at that stage, any plans to include the sailors of the *Victory* as part of the funeral cortège. The *Victory* put in at Spithead, but was ordered to sail to Sheerness to a naval anchorage at the mouth of the river Thames, at which time the body was placed in a lead coffin. Then, on the 21st of the month, Nelson was laid in his own coffin made of wood from the *Orient*, a French battleship blown up during his victorious Battle of the Nile.

So obsessed with the aftermath of Trafalgar were the London-dwelling lovers, as they had become, that the festivities for the season soon upon them had to take second place. Though from Smithfield Market, Constance acquired a truly magnificent turkey, and from Fortnum's in Piccadilly various preserves and chutneys in the hope that she could tempt Lynton's palate. For a man who was little more than skin and bone to be "off his food" was the last thing she wanted. She purchased candied fruits, chocolate, fudge, citrus fruits and freshly baked bread and, as she hurried through the London streets, she thought of the Christmas the year before when they'd gone to the pantomime in Drury Lane. Lynton had seemed at the time not to be in the best of health. But, she had to admit, his condition had vastly deteriorated.

She was now beginning to find her way round the city, and what had earlier been simply names to her were becoming part of a London that she could actually see. Westminster Abbey, the river Thames, street markets, and Bow Street, where she'd seen the horse patrol men—known as 'Robin Redbreasts' because of the distinctive scarlet waistcoats they wore under their blue greatcoats—mounted and on their way to serve writs and carry out arrests on the authority of the magistrates. She'd also seen the poor and destitute, barefooted children, street musicians scraping squeaky viols or blowing wheezy tin whistles. London, she had already decided, was for her a place to visit, not to live, and the sooner she and Lynton could set off for Yorkshire the better. Yet travel during the oncoming months would be difficult, for besides the likelihood of roads becoming impassable because of snowfalls, there was also the physical condition of the invalid to consider. His health would not improve by being exposed to the harsh winter weather. She yearned again for the comforts of Whitby when contrasted with the rented rooms she and Lynton now shared.

Yet Constance put on a brave face. Her father gave her a more-than-generous allowance, and they were together. Even though not legally wed they lived as husband and wife, and at night she would cuddle up to him and, stifling her tears, would enjoy each precious moment. Sometimes he would be too weak to respond to her advances, and they would simply hold hands. How ardent their loving could have been—would have been—were it not for his illness! Constance thought of the courtesans and harlots so well-versed in the art of lovemaking, and the unashamed sexual pleasure and ecstasy of their calling, and at such times would imagine that she herself were one such lady, and would tell herself the man beside her was a shy inexperienced client and that she must take the initiative and guide him to fulfilment and unashamed pleasure. That she had been a virgin only days before, Constance saw rather as a blessing than a hindrance, for they could explore this new experience of lovemaking together, and her hands would search and caress his intimate parts, her whisperings entice and arouse his desires, her kisses provoke ecstasy and—finally—fulfilment.

Oh, she felt truly a wicked woman!

The afternoon was mean and cold, the skies low and malevolent, with scarves of fog wafting from the Esk and creeping insidiously along Church Street and encircling the Town Hall portico, then hovering around Henrietta Street and the abbey steps. Leah stood and looked down over the harbour, the moored ships appearing as ghosts. There was a sudden gentle sea-breeze, and as the swirling mist momentarily cleared, she watched a rigger glide silently by. It was a craft well-known to a select few, for there was always secrecy surrounding its arrival— even more so regarding its cargo—and she thought of certain bottles and jars in Tom's preparation room, and how he had come by them.

How they'd always looked forward to their Christmas festivities! Uncle Nathan, when he'd seen the goose arrive of the dining table, would become suddenly able to feed himself! There had been the excitement of unwrapping presents and...

With sadness, Leah realised that all this was now at an end.

She would not even get to see Tom and Duncan on Christmas Day, for Ashley had arranged that he and Leah should spent Christmas in Scarborough, in some fancy hotel. "Another honeymoon" he called it when the two of them were on their own. Then he'd grow flustered and say he wanted her to have a break from cooking and the like. He wanted to spoil her.

Cooking?—But they had a cook-housekeeper, a parlourmaid and a serving-maid, and also a handyman (whom, on more than one occasion, she'd found "inspecting" the wine cellar, but had thought it best not to tell Ashley). She supposed... she could do some embroidery, or take up painting... or start "collecting things"—if only she could decide what to collect.

Birds eggs? Blue and white china? Snuff boxes?—the choice was hers.

The truth was, she wanted none of them. Married life was all well and good—but what did one do to pass the time? She indulged in thoughts of Christmases past, and viewed the prospect of spending the festive period in some hotel, surrounded by strangers, with caution—even dread!

Sarah thought, too—of childhood Christmases marred by poverty. But more recent and sharper in her mind, the Staithes Christmases, when the Dacres would come home the worse for drink, with a stolen goose or turkey under their arm. There would be the usual arguments, often ending in a fight. Then there was the time when a drunken Cain, boasting what a "big man" he was, had urinated into the kitchen fire and all over the hearthrug.

And there were the Christmases without Cain, when she had felt even more of a prisoner, as she toiled and cooked for an ungrateful father-in-law and his three bachelor sons. Little wonder that they were unwed—who'd want to marry a Dacre?

But, as she once again reminded herself, she was still legally married to Cain. Until he was caught and tried and executed, she was still his wife. And since seeing him in the churchyard, following Stanhope's advice, she was constantly on her guard. Fearful that at any moment he would suddenly appear.

And if he did, whatever would she do?

All very well if Tom were at hand to defend her. But if she were, say, on her way home from visiting Lady Celia, or had just popped out to the grocers for something for the evening meal —what would she do if she came face-to-face with him, and he wanted to—?

But she suppressed her silly notions. There were still things to do before they could sit down to their meal. The roast parsnips just needed glazing, the haunch of venison was "resting", the potatoes were cooked, the jam sponge steaming, the egg custard already made. Time to call the two men in her life, to tell them the meal was ready.

After yet another sightseeing morning, followed by a restful afternoon, they indulged themselves in a romantic evening in one another's arms, vowed eternal love, and finally succumbed to what they laughingly referred to as "forbidden fruit"—and thus did they spend their Christmas Eve.

Christmas morning found them still in the throes of passion. Constance cast lustful eyes over Lynton's naked torso as the tip of her tongue teased the copper-coloured hair that grew in abundance on his chest, then in a deliciously provocative way she went down his tummy to his groin. He stirred and suddenly shivered, then looked out onto the London Street below.

She blew him a kiss. "Merry Christmas, Mr Shaw."

"And to you, Miss Langden. You have made my Christmas morning delightful."

"But what is to become of me?"—and she pursed her lips and gave a most demure, seductive glance at his still-naked body—"for I am a 'ruined woman'."

"You are a temptress, and you have seduced and captivated me. I am your slave—yours to command."

"Then take me, Sir—have your wicked way with me!" And she fell into his arms, her fingers going again to that part of his anatomy that had earlier given her so much pleasure. "But first I must make up the fire if we are to have a traditional Yorkshire Christmas Day lunch, for I need to cook our goose."

He could not let the moment pass. "Constance, darling—I think we've done that, by now."

Chapter 23

The first week in the new year saw the transporting of Nelson's body from Gravesend, escorted by hundreds of boats up-river, to Westminster and Greenwich Hospital.

There, in the painted hall, and now in a gilded casket with lavish decorations celebrating his life and victories, the coffin came to rest and lay open for viewing. The Prince of Wales was the first mourner, paying a private visit before the doors were opened to the general public.

Constance and Lynton were among the many, both high and lowly, who queued for what seemed like hours (and was) to pay their respects. In keeping with the sombre occasion, black hangings draped the vivid wall paintings. Yet brightly coloured shields and coats of arms were permitted to gleam in the glow from hundreds of candles, the coffin being surrounded by trophies, including captured French and Spanish flags. One-by-one the figures filed past, their heads bowed low. Lynton had earlier been dosed with a good measure of linctus to calm his persistent cough, and Constance had with her a phial of oil of peppermint and eucalyptus to sprinkle on a handkerchief to help his breathing, should it be necessary to do so. Yet her lover seemed in good health, being certainly… and she tried hard to control her more-than-mildly erotic thoughts. Such things as she were thinking would come later: not in the painted hall at Greenwich Hospital.

Two days later, on the 8th January, there was the Grand River Procession from Greenwich to London. The river was indeed busy, for a large flotilla of all manner of craft had assembled, including barges owned by the City Livery Companies, resplendent with carved and gilded decorations and colourful banners. As the convoy slowly advanced up the Thames, the escorting vessels fired their guns, the coffin itself having being transported in the royal barge originally built for Charles II. The gilding and paintwork were now, as befitting the occasion, shrouded in black velvet, a large canopy having been erected over the stern, surmounted by black ostrich feathers. Never was a pageant more sorrowful, more in-keeping with the mood of those who beheld it, and after processing through London the funeral cortège arrived at Whitehall Stairs near Westminster.

The following morning found Lynton with a fever. But, determined he should miss nothing, the two of them joined a procession so truly huge that when the head of the column arrived at St Paul's Cathedral, the funeral car, designed to look like the *Victory* and hung with the great naval hero's trophies, had not even left Whitehall. Included in the funeral parade were Greenwich pensioners and Nelson's fellow-officers, plus members of the *Victory* crew. Constance and Lynton stood with the rest of London paying their last respects, oblivious of the January day until, as dusk approached, Nelson's body arrived at the cathedral. There, they later learned, a special lantern mounted with over a hundred individual lamps had been suspended inside the dome, from which hung captured French and Spanish flags. On arrival, the body was placed beneath this lantern. The service itself, simple yet emotional, was performed as part of the usual evensong, as behind the coffin stood his male relatives, including his young nephew, George Matcham.

After evensong the organist played a "Grand Dirge" composed especially for the occasion. And, to add a sense of finality to the ceremony, after the words "earth to earth, ashes to ashes, dust to dust" had been uttered, an arrangement of one of Handel's choruses: *His body is buried in peace—but his name liveth evermore* was sung as the closing anthem. The coffin was lowered into the crypt, the chief herald reading out the full titles of the deceased, ending with a tribute to "the hero who, in the moment of victory, fell, covered with immortal glory". The gold-encrusted coffin was later to be placed in an ornate tomb beneath the dome of St Pauls.

It had been a long, sad day.

From newlywed surgeon and his wife, to well-established apothecary and his wealthy mistress, even to such persons as Lady Celia and her nephew, it promised to be a cruel winter. But to someone living off his wits, needing to remain in hiding among the harbourside scum, forever hungry and cold, life was indeed hard.

More than once had he contemplated stowing away on some ship leaving Whitby heading for no-matter-where, and as he once again considered this possibility, Cain Dacre's thoughts turned not so much to his estranged wife, but to Wilf Gibbons, his father-in-law. Clough Gate, or Clough Farm, or whatever-as-made-no-difference somewhere in Sleights, was only an hour away. If he were to present himself there, he'd probably get a hot meal and even a bed for the night. Anything would be better than his present situation, and he thought about ham and eggs, beef broth and lots of freshly baked bread with lashings of butter washed down with home-brewed ale, home-made apple pie and cream. Oh—the joys of country living.

His expectations however were short-lived, for there was no friendly welcome when finally he reached Far Clough. Just strangers, mucking out cattle, who knew nothing of the man he sought.

"Never heard of Wilf Gibbons—but there's a *Sarah* Gibbons…"

"Who owns this farm and several others nearby… and properties, cottages and the like."

"Oh…?"

"Lives in the big house at Upgang—the one with the high wall and poplar trees…"

"Leastways"—and the farmer's wife gave a smile that spoke of things unsaid—"when she's not staying with the Whitby apothecary."

"She's… a woman of means, then?"

The tenant farmer nodded, and Cain Dacre stood rooted to the spot.

Because of the occasion and the inclement weather, Ashley sent a carriage to collect Tom, Sarah and Duncan, who were to join himself and Leah for an evening's entertainment at the theatre in Skate Lane. A thirtieth birthday, according to his wife, was something to celebrate, and an occasion for herself and Sarah to dress in their finery and dazzle the local populace.

The Richmond Theatre, under the direction and auspices of Samuel Butler, were performing, as part of their winter tour, a play which catered for the enthusiasm and exuberance of child prodigies. They had even engaged the services of Master Williams, the Young Roscuis of York, to appear with the company for two nights, to play the part of Fred in *Lovers' Vows*.

"You wouldn't like to be an actor, would you, when you grow up?" Tom teased.

Duncan pulled a face. "No, I want to be an apothecary and work with you."

"Good lad"—and the waiter brought glasses of champagne, and cordial for the "young gentleman", while Leah and Sarah, the one wearing pale lemon taffeta and a gold silk shawl with long tassels, the other in vivid blue stripes and a fur wrap and ostrich feathers in her hair, posed, waiting for admiration to be bestowed.

"Do you remember the last time we were here?" said Leah. "Constance was with us, and—"

"We'd just become betrothed," Ashley replied. "Yes, I remember it well."

"I was so young and innocent then."

"Well," Tom gave her a saucy wink, "you're still young."

At the end of the entertainment, and after further drinks at the bar, the waiting carriage made its way through the town, over the bridge and along Church Street. There the birthday guests alighted, too busy saying "thank you for a wonderful evening" to each other to notice a figure in the shadows suddenly stir.

"Bitch!" He spat out the word as he watched them enter the Apothecary's. The fine gown and fancy feathers had finally convinced him that the farmer at Far Clough had been correct: his estranged wife had indeed become a woman of means.

Stanhope read the letter a second time, pausing and re-reading lines such as "nor can I stress upon you too much the need for secrecy and absolute confidentiality"—yet though he looked for a hidden meaning, or clues as to her predicament, found none. Except entreaties that he should tell no-one, not even their father. That she had contacted *him* further highlighted speculation regarding the plight of his sister who (for some reason she had failed to mention) was now at an address in York.

Stanhope consulted his diary. The last day of the month, as she suggested, was available for their meeting. He would travel to York by the morning coach, see Constance in the afternoon, hopefully returning to Whitby later that same evening.

He spent the rest of the day speculating. It could be something-and-nothing that she had blown out of all proportion—but that wasn't like his sister. Phrases such as "secrecy and absolute confidentiality" indicated an altogether different scenario.

Chapter 24

She gave a thin, tired smile. "Stanhope, how kind of you to come!"

"Well—your letter obviously gave me cause for concern. As indeed did the fact that you've taken temporary lodgings in York. York of all places! I mean, why—?"

"Stanhope—Mr Langden—this meeting has to be regarded as a 'professional consultation'—and to make it so, then you must in due course present your account for services rendered."

He stared at her: his sister. Then finally he replied, "Certainly, Miss Langden, and you may rest assured that whatever facts you care to divulge will go no further. What passes between the two of us is for our ears alone. Now let us pause… and in your own time tell me what it is that has caused you to contact me."

His sister took a deep breath, then said, "Lynton is dead. He died in my arms. I—I don't know how to begin to…" and she suddenly burst into floods of tears.

"Oh, Connie!"—and he momentarily abandoned the solicitor/client relationship. "I am so very, *very* sorry," he kept repeating. "So very, *very* sorry."

"We were… so looking forward to being husband and wife… but that first afternoon when I went to visit him at the Naval Hospital I knew our time together would be short. Every minute then seemed special… and that's why we—"

"That's all right. Please… take your time."

"—That is why we became lovers. Does that shock you?"

He shook his head.

"Because we were going to get married, it didn't seem wrong, what we were doing… Anyway, you can probably guess what I'm about to tell you."

"That you're *enceinte*—having his child?"

She nodded.

"And you…?"

She shook her head. "Time was precious. Because Lynton was so ill we lived for the moment. A marriage ceremony was the last thing on our minds. So you see, Stanhope, your sister is to become an unmarried mother. The shame will lead papa to an early grave. Oh—what am I to do?"

Her brother thought long and hard. Then he finally said, "We need to consider the future, both for you and your child, and no-one need ever know—"

"But when the child is born—?"

"…Need ever know that you and Lynton Shaw were not husband and wife prior to the child being conceived. You can say, even to papa, that your wedding was a very secretive affair because Lynton was so ill. The business of legally changing your name I can deal with, and any other things, as-and-when they arise. You need to buy a wedding ring and widow's weeds before you return to Whitby."

She stared. "You're being so… *practical*—at a time like *this*—!"

"I'm here to advise you. That is why you invited me."

"But… to tell a deliberate lie!"

"If you don't, your child will be branded a bastard, and you'll be seen as little better than a strumpet"—and he threw up his hands in despair. "Constance, do listen, for God's sake! I'm trying to save both you and your unborn child from back-biting and sniggering. Whitby will be welcoming and kind to a grieving widow. Papa will not bury himself in his library in shame, and you'll be able to hold your head up high. Do believe me. Now, which is it to be? Miss Langden—or Mrs Shaw?"

Constance thought long and hard. "Mrs Shaw!"

"Then, Mrs Shaw, I shall provide you with the necessary documentation. We need to be circumspect: nothing must be left to chance. Let us spend the rest of the afternoon deciding on what—and when—to tell papa. I think it best that you write to inform him you're spending a few days in York, and that you'll be home… shall we say, at the weekend?"

She nodded.

"And this 'professional consultation', as you wished it to be, is now at an end."

Taking her hand, he said in a completely altered voice, "Your secret is safe with me, Connie."

A sudden snowfall, making the road impassable, necessitated an overnight stay in York—and Stanhope returned to Whitby to the distressing news that Malahide O'Connor, on leaving one of the quayside taverns, had been the victim of a vicious attack. His assailant (and this came as no surprise to Stanhope but he thought it best to keep his counsel) had been a man with a purple stain across his hand. O'Connor had been taken to the dispensary in Sanders Yard. His condition was said to be grave.

She cut a pathetic figure as she alighted from the coach, drew back her veil, and beheld a father who stared at her as though he were in a dream.

"Constance, my dear"—and he shook himself. His daughter… in deep mourning?

"Oh, papa"—and she smiled through her tears as she began her well-rehearsed tale. "I needed to get away from London, yet I felt I had to be on my own, to come to terms with my great loss. Hence my stay in York. Oh, papa—a bride and a widow in the same month! Life can be so cruel!"

"Oh, my child. My poor, poor Constance."

"Lynton was so ill, so very, very ill. Yet brave to the last. He will surely be in heaven." And with downcast eyes she murmured, "God chooses only the most perfect flowers for His garden."

"Let's… get you home. And then, when you're ready you must tell me… everything. Oh Constance, I am so very, very sorry."

"Because Lynton was so ill, we couldn't wait for the St Mary's wedding you'd always promised me, when I'd walk down the aisle on your arm and—oh, papa, I feel so wretched!"

"We'll… this has come as a complete shock, my dear. Let's get you home—"

"And I must let the rest of the family know, because—"

"All that will come later, when you're ready."

She held his arm as they made their way to the Langden residence, her father worried lest they should meet any of their friends, who would start asking questions. Still, he reasoned, the sooner people knew, the easier it would be for her.

Married—then widowed, within such a short space of time! It was unthinkable! So very, very tragic.

By great good fortune, they'd no sooner turned the key in the lock than Stanhope appeared. When the tragic circumstances were recounted to him, he took charge of the situation. He would inform the other members of the family, and supervise any formal announcements that needed to be made. Any "legal loose-ends" that needed tying up he would deal with—Constance need have no worries on that score.

"Oh, thank you, Stanhope!"

"It is the least I can do. And any affairs that may arise in connection with Lynton's estate—I trust you'll let me deal with those as well."

"Thank you, son." The old man placed a hand on his shoulder. "And while you're attending to all that, I'll look after Constance."

Good as his word, Stanhope called on Westwood and Ashley, after which Leah went to tell Tom and Sarah the sad news.

When Stanhope returned to his chambers, his clerk had further revelations about the other business. Malahide O'Connor was dead—and the search was on for the man who had attacked him. Notices were being posted around the town: *Cain Dacre. Wanted for Murder!*

Stanhope went to visit Tom and Sarah himself. "You must be on your guard, for he could have knowledge of your whereabouts and may try to contact you"—and Stanhope looked around him as he spoke. "When I leave, lock the doors. It seems that he's living rough, sleeping where he can, but frequently to be seen on the quayside. Even as we speak, the town militia are searching boats, ships—anywhere he may try to hide."

Sarah asked the obvious question. "And what if they don't find him?"

"They will," Stanhope assured her. "Yet it may be expedient—as a 'precautionary' measure only, you understand—for you to leave Whitby until such a time as he's safely behind bars."

She looked helplessly at Tom. "But where will I go?"

"Leave it to me"—and Stanhope hurried away. He had much to do.

Chapter 25

The following morning, with a brusqueness befitting his station, Stanhope, with Constance at his side, called at the Whitby apothecary's.

His usual sombre attire was eclipsed by that of his sister acting the grieving widow. Over her gloves she wore a large mourning ring and, clasped in her hands, was a prayer book. Her head was bowed, for she was in truth carrying the sorrows of the world upon her shoulders.

Some thirty minutes later, with Stanhope still in attendance, the two of them in a slow, dignified manner walked along to the nearby tavern, where the York-bound coach was waiting. The "widow" bade farewell to her brother and boarded the coach.

After seeing his charge safely off on her journey, Stanhope went about his business.

Tom and Duncan opened their doors for their morning customers, who came and left. And, slipping out amongst those who left… went Constance Langden—no longer dressed as a widow!

At the *Hare and Hounds* the coach drew in and halted. While the travellers were able to partake of the hospitality of the inn-keeper and his good wife, the team of horse was changed.

Sarah sipped her cordial and was about to make herself comfortable on the oak settle when a man standing near the bar with his back to her suddenly spun round.

She felt the colour drain from her cheeks. Her head began to swim and, as she slumped forward, strong arms reached out to grab hold of her.

"And where are you goin', mi fine lady?" he spat the words out, his face up against hers, madness flashing in his eyes. Her breathing grew laboured and she silently mouthed the word "Cain" unable to speak his name. He stood leering.

Then, not wishing to draw attention to himself, but at the same time keeping a tight hold on her wrist, he sat down beside her. She wanted to scream—to cry out for all to hear—but she was struck dumb.

Stanhope's planning and subterfuge had come to nothing. Now she was on her own—and at the mercy of her estranged husband.

She swallowed, then finally managed to speak. "How did you know… it was me was on the coach?"

"D'yer think me daft?" He pointed to his temple. "I've got it all up 'ere. I know you've bin carryin' on wi' that Whitby quack. I've been watchin' the pair o' you for days, lady, and—"

Abruptly he stopped. "Somebody's lookin' this way. You start talkin' all pretty, like."

"But how did you know?" she repeated her earlier question.

"Simple. The real widow woman, the one as came into the apothecary's with the smart toff, was taller than the one he later led to the coach. I put two and two together, walked past the Custom House where a horse was just being tied up—and when the rider went inside… I 'elped meself."

"And followed the coach, so's you could—"

"Come to an' arrangement." A nasty smile. "I've bin 'earin' rumours… that you've inherited a fortune! An' the way I sees it… a wife's wealth belongs to 'er 'usband. Yet I'm reduced to beggin' while you're behavin' like Lady Bountiful."

"That's not the way of it, Cain—besides, you're a wanted man, and…"

"…Desperate!" He finished the sentence for her.

Sarah looked around her, toward the rest of the travellers who were now moving toward the door. They couldn't just leave her there—not with Cain Dacre!

"Ready in five minutes, Ma-am," the coachman said to her.

"'Lady's 'ad a change of plan," Cain spoke up for her. "She'll nooan be travellin' any further." And feeling something sticking in her side, she saw the barrel of a gun. "Tell 'im," he snarled, "or I'll go to Whitby and blow yer apothecary's brains out."

Sarah saw the maniacal look in his eyes, the same as she'd seen that night when he'd bashed their baby against the wall. Finally she managed to say, "that's correct. I'll not be travelling any further."

The coachman look puzzled, but could do nothing else than accept what she said. Besides, it was time they were away, for precious minutes wasted at the outset of a journey could multiply into hours before the coach reached its destination, and also there was the threat of further snowfalls.

After a "well if you're sure, Ma-am…" the driver took his place, a horn sounded, and the coach was away.

A now-petrified Sarah asked her captor, "What are you going to do, Cain—what happens now?"

"You got some money? I need a drink."

She opened her purse and he quickly snatched it. "This'll do"—and he held aloft a guinea, then flicked it in the air. "But I'll keep the rest. Now, I'm 'avin' a measure of ale at Tom Metcalfe's expense. I fancy 'ee owes me that at least, seein' as 'ee's bin beddin' my wife every night, little whore that she is. And then… well, we're goona—"

"...Yes?"

"Don't 'assle me," he snarled. "I'm tryin' ter think."

"When I don't arrive in York it'll arouse suspicion," Sarah warned. "There'll be questions, and it'll come out that you—"

"Shut up!"

"You're a wanted man, Cain, after what you did to Malahide O'Connor—there's posters all over town. You won't escape this time."

"Pint of yer best ale, landlord." Cain smiled at the man, who was now giving them curious looks, and Sarah again felt the gun in her side.

Soon the worse for drink, he stared into an empty tankard as Sarah tried again. "You see Cain, I don't think even you know what you rightly want, but—"

"To get away. Make a fresh start."

"But you'd never—"

"Not without money. But... you're a lady of means!"

"I couldn't just lay my hands on it like that. It's in property and the like."

"The apothecary, then?—Look, I need enough to start a new life, a long way away."

"It'd have to be."

"Another country... oh, I dunno. But there's one thing"—and he clutched her arm—"you're stayin' with me till I'm safe. Now, let's leave this place afore they become suspicious."

Outside there was a fine covering of snow as he pushed her up onto the mare's back, then mounted himself. She could smell alcohol on his breath and the stink of sweat from his body. She wanted to be sick.

A strange sight they made as they crossed the moors: she in deepest mourning, her companion the worse for drink, cursing and trying to control the horse with one hand on the reins, the other constantly doing battle with her wafting widow's weeds. After several miles, Cain took a turning off the main road, and Sarah realised that they were heading toward the coast, and that they would eventually come to the road that led toward Staithes.

The very thought of it filled her with dread.

The ground rose sharply, and through the skeletal winter trees Sarah saw to her right a building perched on top of the cliffs, silhouetted against a pewter sky that merged into an equally pewter sea. Outside the *Mulgrave Inn* Cain tethered the horse, then in a dangerous voice warned, "any funny business"—and he touched his pistol to complete his sentence. She nodded obediently.

"Then walk in front—but for God's sake get rid o' that bloody silly 'at."

"What'll I do with it?"

"Oh—carry the damned thing if you must... only cum on, I want a drink."

Inside the raftered room, Sarah paused to adjust her eyes to the sudden gloom. At the far end of the room, in boisterous conversation, were three men, their rough words mingling with the pungent smell of their tobacco.

Cain pointed to the wooden settle. "Sit!" Then, fingering the coins he'd earlier extracted from her purse he thought, "what the hell, why settle for common ale when there's something better?" And like a man coming into sudden wealth he gave the landlord a supercilious look. "Brandy—yer best."

For the next hour he steadily consumed tumbler after tumbler, the warm sweetness of the amber liquid doing little to soothe his tongue, or release his victim from his constant gaze. He sat, stupefied, and no longer attempting to keep his hand hidden from view, stared around him, careless of—indeed hoping for—trouble. But, much to his annoyance, the men were ignoring him.

Turning to Sarah, new mischief in his mind, he suddenly announced, "Right Lady—time thee an' me were away."

He rose unsteadily and, wreathed in brandy fumes, grabbed Sarah's arm and steered her towards the door. Outside, the unexpected rays of sunlight now dancing on the sea caused his to put his hands to his eyes to shield them from the glare.

In that instant Sarah made her move, pushing him with all her might toward the rain-butt. And not even pausing to consider which direction to take, thinking only of putting some distance between herself and her captor, she hitched up her long skirts and began running toward the cliffs. She heard him roar and curse as he collided with the barrel. She ran as though her life depended on it. Her breathing became more difficult and, glancing over her shoulder, she saw that he was gaining on her.

In the distance were some cottages. Madly she reasoned that if she were to head in that direction she could get help, for surely there'd be some men there who could fight him off. She could hear the ground ringing from the sound of his boots as he raced toward her. He was gaining, getting nearer and nearer. She screamed and ran the harder.

"Stupid cow"—and she was almost jerked off her feet as she felt his hands and arms grab wildly at her. He caught the brim of the hat she'd been wearing and, as he pulled it toward him, Sarah, without thinking, released her grip on it.

The wide brim and long trails of scarf slipped from her fingers and, as her pursuer reeled backwards, Sarah, as though in a dream, watched helplessly as he staggered toward the edge of the cliff. She both saw and heard his body strike the rock face and bounce off, heard his agonising screams and watched her hat, now seemingly suspended in the air, gently float down after him, long swirling trails of gauze like fiends from Hades waving their black arms to welcome him.

She stared at the body sprawled at the foot of the cliffs far below. Nothing moved, save the waves lapping against his head—and Sarah realised she was free!

Free from the ordeal she had just endured… but more importantly, there was now no possibility of Cain spoiling the happiness that could be hers and Tom's. They could live together free from fear that he would suddenly appear… and now she was a widow, they could marry!

If Tom would say, "Let's get married"—she could now say, "Yes".

She stood watching the sea coming in over Cain, then receding, as two revenue men caught sight of him, gave him a cursory examination and pronounced him dead. Then one noticed the purple hand and, seeing their chance to claim the reward offered for him, slung his body across one of their horses.

That evening, in the warmth and safety of the apothecary's, Sarah told her tale. And when she had finished, Duncan threw his arms around her. "Oh mum—I'm so pleased that you're safe. I do love you, you know"—and that seemed to her the perfect ending to the day.

Epilogue

Only months after Cain's death, Tom and Sarah were wed. St Mary's bells pealed over the town, for indeed it was a joyous occasion.

Later that year Constance gave birth to a son, Maximilian, and Leah and Ashley were the proud parents of a baby boy they called Richard. Time marched on, and in 1810 there was an addition to the Metcalfe family: a baby daughter, Sarah Louise. Beyond the boundaries of Whitby, across the sea that guards her coastline, Napoleon married the Archduchess Marie Louise of Austria, while in Poland was born a child who was to have such an influence on the musical life of the civilised world: Frédéric Chopin.

The following year King George III was declared insane, the Prince of Wales becoming Prince Regent. The year also heralded the birth of another composer, Franz Liszt, and on Christmas Day, 1811 Tom and Sarah were blessed with another daughter, Angele. Then, some four years later, came a son, Jack.

Duncan, now a young man, and no longer an apprentice, looked on this new addition to the family as his own son and doted on him ceaselessly. Both Tom and Sarah had been kind and loving toward the workhouse orphan, and this was his way of returning their affection. Duncan seemed now to have taken over the running of the apothecary's and was soon to wed and set up home in a yard off nearby Baxtergate. His friend, Lord Percival, died, alas, before inheriting his Earldom.

Cousins Maximilian and Richard became inseparable, attended the same private school and, years later, the two of them went to St Barts to study medicine together.

When in 1820 King George III died, Tom's thoughts turned to uncle Nathan and his earlier talk of assassination. But he had been a harmless, confused old man. A kind old man who, all those years ago, had taken-in the orphaned sister and brother who had presented themselves on his doorstep, and Tom would remember that so much, so very much, had happened since. Much had changed, not only in the world at large, but in the lives of himself and Leah, and even in Whitby: this fishing town on the North Yorkshire coast that had become their home; and in the beautiful surrounding moors.

In the next decade there was talk of a Whitby to Pickering railway line, with an original estimate of £120,000 for its construction (the eventual estimate being £226,000)—and an Act of Parliament for the construction of the line was passed in May, 1833.

The following month, eighteen-year-old Jack, now a handsome young man, fell in love—the first of many such adventures. Yet he was to discover that Adonis-like features such as his were not always an asset. He led a wonderful, charmed life until, at the age of twenty-five (and just as his father had done so many years before), he chanced to venture up the coast and stumble upon a certain fishing village. There, prey to Cupid, he met a girl called Lavinia and fell hopelessly in love.

But her two brothers, seeking retribution for their sister having been seduced—*defiled by a stranger*—lay in wait for him one night and, dragging him to the scaurs of rocks at the mouth of the beck where it disgorged into the sea, they bludgeoned him to death.

Only weeks later, a child was born to the twenty-year-old Lavinia. The unwed mother held the infant to her breast and wondered what the future would hold for him. She had already decided on a name. In keeping with the Dacre family and its Huguenot extraction, but also to commemorate the child's father, he would be called Jacques.

Jacques Dacre of Steeas—it had a good sound.